drummer girl

drummer girl

KAREN BASS

Edited by Laura Peetoom
Designed by Michel Vrana
Typeset by Susan Buck

Library and Archives Canada Cataloguing in Publication

Bass, Karen, 1962-
Drummer girl / Karen Bass.

ISBN 978-1-55050-462-0

I. Title.

PS8603.A795D78 2011 jC813'.6 C2011-903836-6

2517 Victoria Avenue
Regina, Saskatchewan
Canada S4P 0T2
www.coteaubooks.com

Available in Canada from:
Publishers Group Canada
2440 Viking Way
Vancouver, British Columbia
Canada V6V 1N2
Available in the US from:
Orca Book Publishers
www.orcabook.com
1-800-210-5277

Printed in Canada
10 9 8 7 6 5 4 3 2 1

Coteau Books gratefully acknowledges the financial support of its publishing program by: the Saskatchewan Arts Board, the Canada Council for the Arts, the Government of Canada through the Canada Book Fund, the Government of Saskatchewan through the Creative Economy Entrepreneurial Fund, the Association for the Export of Canadian Books and the City of Regina Arts Commission.

Canada Council for the Arts
Conseil des Arts du Canada
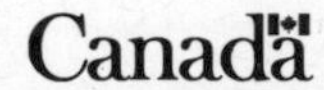

Saskatchewan Ministry of Tourism, Parks, Culture and Sport

City of Regina

To Mom,
for always encouraging my artistic endeavours.

1 | off beat

Sid stood rooted to the lawn and considered that this might be the worst idea in the history of Edwards High School. Okay, maybe not in the whole school's history. But definitely in hers.

The house before her throbbed with an insistent bass beat, an umbilical cord of sound that wouldn't release her. When the open windows began to pump out a wicked drum solo, Sid groaned quietly and took a hesitant step forward, drawn by the pulse.

Why had she let Taylor bully her into this? He'd said that all the guys from The Fourth Down were going to be here and it was her best chance out of school to tell them she wanted to be their drummer. She'd argued it was going to be a jock party. Beer guzzling, muscle-flexing jocks with cheerleader girlfriends in micro-minis and skimpy tops. "Yeah," Taylor had sighed. "I wish I could go. Live it for both of us, Sid. It's gonna be a blow-out."

So here she was. But instead of being eager to join the

throng inside, she gaped at the shadows moving across the windows.

Someone bumped her shoulder as he brushed by. He half turned, then pointed at Sid's T-shirt. "In Flames. What's that? How you're going down tonight?" He burst into laughter, apparently overcome by his own wit, and walked away. Stumbled, actually, beer bottle in hand. Sid managed to offer him a half-hearted sneer.

The music melted into a sickly pop tune with no beat to speak of. It made Sid's feet want to pound out a retreat. But the chance to talk to the guys in the band kept her in place. She stuffed her hands in her cargo pockets and mentally began to gather her courage.

A black wall materialized in front of her. She looked up to see Narain grinning. "Hey, Sid. You look ready to bail. Taylor warned me you might."

That did it. She was out of here. She gave a smile that was all grimace and tried to step around him. He showed why he was a great basketball guard, sidestepping to block her again. Before she could feint past him, he grabbed her shoulders, turned her around and began marching her toward the party house.

"I don't know why I'm friends with you and Tay. Let me go, you thug," Sid said. "Just because you're taller than me doesn't mean you can push me around."

"I'm doing it for your own good, Sid. Come on. Not only is TFD inside, but I heard that someone's looking for you. You know you'll regret it if you don't find out who it is."

Sid barely refrained from rolling her eyes. “Why don’t you just tell me who it is?”

“’I don’t know. I heard it from someone who heard it from someone.”

Sid dug in her heels and brought them both to a stop. “Didn’t you ever play that gossip game in elementary? You know, someone whispers something, it goes around the circle and always ends up way different from that first whisper. I’m going to walk in that house and find out there is no *someone*.”

“Sure there is. I trust my source.”

Sid glared up at her friend. “You can never trust a snitch.”

Narain laughed. His teeth flashed white in his milk chocolate face. “You’re scared.”

“Do you blame me? That’s a houseful of jocks. They tackle things for fun.”

“You swing the meanest hammer in carpentry class. They’re the ones who should be scared.”

A snort escaped out Sid’s nose. This time she did roll her eyes. “Fine. I’ll go in. But if I don’t find the band, secret admirer or not, I’m leaving without you.”

Narain grinned. “Lelah is probably already there, waiting for me to dance her off her feet, so I can’t say I’d notice you leaving anyway, especially if there’s a slow song playing.”

Sid hit him on the shoulder. “Jerk.”

The sprawling house was set deep in a large lot, and the noise didn’t start getting loud until they were halfway up the long sidewalk. Which was likely why no neighbours had called the cops. When Narain opened the door, the music and voices rolled over them. People were shouting to be heard. Narain didn't try to compete. Instead he motioned for Sid to take a walk around. She nodded, suddenly feeling too tongue-tied to talk, even if she wanted to. Narain wedged his way through a cluster of laughing guys on his way to the makeshift dance floor in what looked to be a dining room with the table pushed to the side.

Sid tried to scope the place. She wasn't short, but 5'6" wasn't tall enough to see anything in this crowd. A slow song wafted from the dance floor. No doubt as to what Narain was doing now. Sid sighed and moved down a hallway that seemed to separate the two halves of the house. She recognized a few faces from her classes, a few more from the sports team portraits she'd seen in the school paper, but no one she ever talked to besides Narain. Where would the band members hang out? Rocklin, the leader, was a football player. Was the party segregated by sports teams?

Half a dozen giggling girls tumbled out of a bathroom and forced Sid up against the wall. They didn't notice, turning to wave at some guys near the front door. Off to the left somewhere, the chant of "Chug, chug, chug," made Sid wonder where the cameras were. This was the kind of high school party you saw in movies; they weren't supposed to really happen.

The doorway the chanting had come from was completely clogged. Rocklin was tall but even on her tiptoes Sid didn't spot him inside. She thought she glimpsed Wes Remichuk, which was reason enough to look elsewhere. The hallway reeked of beer. She kept inching toward the back of the house, hoping now to find some fresh air. She glanced down a hallway to what looked to be bedrooms, and veered the other way.

Shrieks caused the crowd around Sid to surge toward an open door, carrying her along. She stumbled onto a stone patio. Her eyes widened at the sight of girls jostling each other and falling, fully clothed, into a kidney-shaped pool while guys stood beside the water and hooted. No doubt hoping some of the girls weren't wearing bras.

Someone walked by and pushed a beer into Sid's hands. She almost dropped it before her fingers found a grip. The bottle felt like a shield. If she held it, no one would push anything else at her. Last September, she and Taylor had renewed their vow to not be stupid about booze. Taylor's cousin had been killed by a drunk driver, so he was kind of touchy on the subject. Sid figured she drummed better when her head was clear.

Where was the band? Or the guy who was supposedly interested? She leaned against the wall under a motion-sensor light and studied the group by the pool, thankful none of the oglers looked her way. No one looked her way. Was she invisible?

Maybe she'd dressed wrong. Any of the girls she'd seen were wearing jeans and tight tops, some with midriffs showing. No band T-shirts. *But I like In Flames. Daniel Svensson is an awesome speed drummer.*

Feeling more than ever that she didn't belong at this party, Sid swung around the empty side of the pool. From the patio, three steps led down to a long stretch of grass. Sid settled on the middle step and set the beer bottle between her sneakers. She needed to think, to figure out how to find the band in that chaos. Was it too much to hope that they might show up on the patio? As for Mr. Interested... He could find her or not, it was up to him.

She took a sip of beer and wrinkled her nose at the taste. Behind her, a guy whooped. This was followed by a massive splash. The girls screamed some more – why didn't they just get out? – and a guy shouted that they should all skinny dip. This suggestion was met with yells of "You do it," and "We need more beer!"

Talking to Rocklin in school was looking better and better. The strains of a Metallica song floated out from the house. Sid tapped her knee to the beat.

A foot scrapped on stone, just behind Sid. Mr. Interested? Her fingers froze, then lowered to grip her knee. Don't look nervous, she thought, but her grip didn't loosen. Someone in shorts that topped impossibly long legs sat beside her. Smooth, hairless legs.

A slightly husky voice said, "I'm glad you came."

Sid turned her head. She knew that slender face, straight blond hair that was usually tied in a pony tail but tonight hung loose. Volleyball team. Sid searched her memory for a name. Joanne. That was it. She offered a smile. "Yeah. I heard someone was looking for me..." She glanced over her shoulder, expecting to see some shy guy hanging back.

Joanne's look softened. "I thought you knew. It was me."

2 | rudiments

Sid struck her crash cymbal. Hard. *Clang-ang-ang!*

She had practised quietly for over an hour, covering the rudiments, but now she vented her feelings in a storm of sound. Under her touch, the drums released a wild rhythm that vibrated through the air, through her skin, through her bones into her core. She played by instinct, every solo she'd ever practised mixing and sifting and sliding into new variations.

Devin would have known how to handle that party last night, how to play it cool. All she had wanted was to let Rocklin know she'd like to try out as The Fourth Down's new drummer. Those guys were the suns of cool and everyone else revolved around them. With his basketball skills, Narain was closer to the centre; she was more like Neptune, on the outskirts but given the nod. (How much of that was because everyone knew she was Devin's sister?) Today she felt as rejected as Pluto, downgraded by experts, no longer a planet.

Her drum kit wasn't big, only five pieces plus cymbals. She knew where each drum was without looking so she played with her eyes slitted, the drums vague shadows in her vision. The sound rose, fell, rose again. Each phrase longer and more intense, until there was no ebb – nothing but the thunder of the bass, the rattle of the toms punctuated by cymbal crashes. Her arms ached. She kept drumming.

The rhythm consumed her. Seeped from the earth, through the basement and the soles of her feet. Surged through her hands. She was the beat's instrument –

A towel hit Sid in the face. She almost fell off her throne. Her foot jerked forward to restore balance, striking the bass drum pedal. A single boom echoed through the room.

Sid breathed hard. She laid her sticks on the snare drum, plucked the towel off her lap, wiped the sweat from her eyes and peered at Taylor. "What're you doing? You scared the crap out of me."

More sweat dripped into her eyes. She wiped it away, then towelled her hair. She could feel a tiny rivulet running down her spine and rubbed the back of her T-shirt. The movement made her realize how sore her arms were.

Taylor stood in the middle of the room with his hands shoved in the pockets of his leather jacket and shook his head slowly.

"What?" she snapped.

"That was really...intense. I don't know if it was music, but it sure was intense."

"What's that? Your word of the day?"

He grinned. "Sure. So what's on your mind that has you so *intense?* Or should I say tense?"

The tone was serious but the grin balanced it, made the question less of a threat. Sid stepped from behind her drums and flung herself on the old green sofa that hunkered between the only two windows in the room. Her dad had added storm windows on the outside hoping to muffle the sound of her drums so their neighbour didn't complain.

She laid her forearm across her eyes and thought about his question.

"Does it have anything to do with the party last night? Wish I could've gone. Family gigs are boring. Narain said he walked with you into the house but lost track of you after that."

"He only had eyes for Lelah."

"Ha! True. Did you get to talk to one of the guys from TFD?"

"No. I couldn't even find them."

"Then why? Wait, let me guess. Did some Mr. Mysterious want to hook up?"

Sid heard the grin in his voice. "No. But Ms. Mysterious did." No response to that. Sid kept her arm firmly in place. It was easier to talk in the dark. "She thought I was gay because I...hit things. I'd never thought of carpentry and drumming as hitting things. I'd been so pumped up to get to talk to the band that it threw me. I brushed her off and left." *Threw* – hah. The incident had freaked her out, but she wasn't going to tell anyone that.

Taylor still didn't respond. She rolled onto her side and tucked her arm under her head. Taylor now sat cross-legged on the hideous red shag rug that she could never talk her dad into replacing. With elbows on knees, he propped his chin on folded hands. His expression was blank. His expression was never blank. Guys always tried to get him to play poker because his face was so easy to read. Fortunately for him and his cash, he knew it.

She propped herself up on her elbow. "You don't seem surprised that some volleyball chick thought I might want to date."

"What do you want me to say, Sid?"

"Do you think I'm gay?"

"Does it matter?"

"I guess not, but why do people think I should be? Why do *you* think I should be?"

"I don't know. You just aren't interested in, you know, girl stuff. *Any* girl stuff. You don't even have any friends who are girls."

Sid glanced down at her band T-shirt and baggy cargoes. Girl stuff. Did Taylor mean clothes and makeup and all that? What was wrong with the way she dressed? It was the same way Devin dressed. And it wasn't like she had a mom around to teach her. "So? Girls are interested in all sorts of things. It's like how Narain says that sometimes people will be surprised he doesn't have an accent because they think he looks like he should. Well, I should be able to dress or act any way I want without someone deciding it means something it doesn't."

Taylor's expression rippled with uncertainty. He straightened and shrugged. "No big deal, Sid. Now Ms. Mysterious knows you're not interested."

"Yeah. You're right." Sid swung into a sitting position and braced her hands on the seat of the sofa. Her shoulders were throbbing from the extended workout. So were her wrists, and bending them sent sharp pains up her arms, so she leaned back and rubbed them. Her mind jumped back to The Fourth Down. "Now how am I supposed to get the band's attention? Only the lead guitar is in our grade and I don't have any classes with him. They're totally unapproachable at school unless you're, well, way cooler than I am. That party was my big chance and I blew it because I panicked."

"There'll be more parties."

"But they're looking for a drummer *now*. I'm so sick of practising in the basement, Tay. It was great when Devin was home and I could jam with his band, but since he left for college it's been brutal. I've got to get in with TFD. I'm good enough now. I'm ready to play. Really *play*." She sighed.

"I don't know if TFD's the best choice..."

"But they *are* the best, around here anyway. And that's what I want: a shot at being best."

He looked skeptical. "They're really into that rock 'n roll party image." Everyone knew TFD's drummer had been drunk when he'd slammed into that light standard. Taylor had been friends with the guy back in elementary school and they'd stayed friendly. The funeral had shaken Taylor up, having happened less than a year after his cousin died the same way.

Sid searched for words to assure him that she'd never fall into that; she only wanted to play. Before she could speak,

Taylor pushed to his feet. "While you're planning your big break I gotta show you something." He tugged at his jeans as a smile played at the corners of his mouth.

Sid stood, relieved he'd changed the subject. With or without his help, she'd find a way to get in tight with the band. She rolled her shoulders and stretched her hands toward the low tiled ceiling, almost touching it.

Taylor laughed. "Next time you beat the hell out of your drums, you might wanna wear a different shirt."

Hands still above her head, Sid eyed her white T-shirt and armpit stains the size of dinner plates. "Yeah. I see what you mean. Rush let me down." She sniffed. "Don't get too close."

He laughed again and headed for the stairs. "You can rinse off before we go out."

"Are we going out?"

He glanced over his shoulder, tripped on the bottom step and fell forward with a loud "oof." Sid suppressed a smile. Taylor was the clumsiest guy she knew. He always laughed along if anyone laughed at him, but she knew it bugged him sometimes. The more he tried to be coordinated, the more spectacularly he failed. Sid still cringed to recall her one attempt to teach Taylor to play the drums.

They clambered up the stairs and into the kitchen. Taylor said, "Hey, Mr. J." That's what he always called Sid's dad, even though their last name was Crowley. J for James.

"Hey, yourself, Taylor. Got Thor to stop making thunder, did you?"

"Funny, Dad." Sid glanced at the automatic

coffeemaker. "On what, your fourth cup? I thought you said you were cutting back."

"I am." He snapped the newspaper and turned the page. "Usually I've had six cups by now."

"Four's probably good for the day then, right?" Before James could answer, Sid removed the carafe from the hot plate and dumped the rest of the coffee down the sink. "You're the one who told me caffeine's hard on the stomach." She eyed the roll of antacid tablets by his cup but didn't say anything. He knew she thought he should go to the doctor.

James only snapped the paper again. "Don't you two have somewhere to go?"

"Yup," Taylor answered. "As soon as Sid showers."

Sid took the hint. Ten minutes later she was back in the kitchen where Taylor and James were discussing the cars for sale in the classifieds.

Sid cleared her throat to get their attention, "Where are we going, Taylor?"

He smiled. "Trust me."

"Guys always say that just before they get you into trouble."

"I don't get you into trouble..." His brow wrinkled. "Intentionally."

James laughed. Taylor added, "Mr. J knows my plan so everything's cool."

Sid's dad nodded. Taylor smiled at her as he passed, bumped his shoulder against a corner and recovered with a quick sidestep. Sid followed at a safe distance, in case Taylor rebounded off something. When they reached the sidewalk, she jogged a few steps to catch up.

"Not going to tell me?" she asked.

"We're going to my place."

"Three whole houses away from home. How will I survive the adventure?"

"With your acid tongue ready to cut through any obstacle."

"Acid tongue. That's harsh."

Taylor grinned. "You should join the Fantastic Four. No villain could stand against you."

"But wouldn't that put the original four out of a job?"

"Hm. You're right. Guess you better stay on as my sidekick, instead."

"What? I thought you were mine."

Taylor grinned again. They reached his house and were halfway up the driveway when Sid noticed the lump draped by a canvas tarp. "Your bike is out of the garage?"

"Yup. Dad and I finished it last night after the birthday party."

"I didn't think you'd ever get it running." Part of her had *hoped* they'd never get it running. Clumsy as he was on two feet, what would he be like on a motorized vehicle that only had two wheels? She almost shuddered at the thought.

Taylor flung the tarp off with the flashiness of a magician. "Ta da!"

Sid blinked and said the first thing that came to mind. "Fenders are still a little rusty."

"Details, details. You won't find any rust on the engine." He tossed her one of two helmets that were on the seat.

She caught it and hugged it against her stomach. "You expect me to ride that thing?"

"We'd look stupid pushing it, especially wearing helmets."

"I'm not so sure about this, Tay."

He put his grey helmet on and fastened the strap. He zipped up his leather jacket. "Why not? I have my licence. And my folks made me take that motorcycle safety course."

"But...you're still you."

He scowled. "Thanks for the vote of confidence." He mounted the bike and wedged the kickstand into place with his heel. "You gonna be my sidekick on this adventure or not?"

Sid sighed and ran her hand over the helmet. Shiny black. Taylor had even put a Metallica sticker on it for her. She slipped on the helmet before she could second-guess herself. Taylor was smiling as he kick-started the bike, which roared to life, immediately subsiding to a quiet rumble.

Taylor patted the seat behind him and she got on, nodding when he showed her the foot pegs. *We're going to crash and die on the first corner.*

He glanced back and said, "Ready?" Sid bit her lip and nodded again.

She'd ridden a few times before on bikes, usually with Devin's friends. Never with Taylor, the clumsiest guy she knew. Her heart began to flutter erratically against her ribs. She reached around his waist and laced her fingers together.

This was going to hurt. So much.

The things a person did for her best friend.

Maybe I'll just break a leg. If it's my left leg I'll still be able to play my drums.

Taylor revved the engine and started with a lurch. Sid squeezed her eyes shut. When they bumped through the gutter and into the street, she opened them. They cruised past her house and she wondered if she'd ever see that moss-green trim again. Puke green, she called it when she was trying to bug her dad. *He agreed to this? Could stomach problems drive a guy insane?*

Taylor took it easy until the end of their block. He swung left and increased speed. So far, so good. He kept the bike steady. Sid started to relax and enjoy the wind in her face and the rumble vibrating through her legs and stomach. She didn't pay attention when he turned onto another street.

Then she glimpsed the S-curve ahead. They were on Jackson Drive, the most crooked road around. Fear tried to crowd back into her mind. She willed herself to stay calm, though her fingers started hurting from their vice-grip. She could imagine Taylor smiling as he sped up a bit more. Though she tried not to, Sid tensed as they hit the first curve. Taylor swept the bike around it like he'd been doing it forever.

Maybe he had finally found something that could overcome his klutzy nature. They cruised through the second curve with equal grace.

Sid freed one hand and pumped the air. "Taylor Janzen, you rock!"

3 | rimshot on a high-pitched snare

The smell of cedar tickled her nose as Sid caressed the lining of the chest she'd been working on for almost two months. This was the best thing she'd ever made. She wondered if she could find some excuse to not give it to her cousin as a wedding gift.

"Nice job on the lining," Mr. Franklin said from right behind her. Sid flinched but managed not to jump. He tended to sneak up on students, which wasn't so great when someone was operating the jigsaw or sander. But otherwise he was a decent carpentry teacher. He let students pick almost any project they wanted. Within reason. Last year he refused a student who wanted to build a lake cottage.

Mr. Franklin said, "Have you decided if you're going to stain it?"

"No. I like the pine exterior. I'll just give it a few coats of varnish. Satin finish."

Mr. Franklin nodded and strode across the shop to where two guys were arguing over whose turn it was to use the router.

Sid stood and brushed sawdust from her knees. It was a good thing carpentry was her last class. All day she'd felt eyes drilling into her, but she could never catch anyone looking at her. It had been unnerving. By the time this class had rolled around she'd felt like she was a tightly strung wire ready to snap. But working with wood was almost as soothing as playing the drums.

Taylor appeared at her side. "Hey, Sid. Done the chest yet?"

She narrowed one eye. "Don't you have English this block?"

"We're working on essays. I asked to go to the library."

Sid glanced around. "I can see where you'd be confused. Books. Wood. Same source."

"I'm doing a good deed, checking up on my sidekick. I saw you in the hall before class but was going the other way. You looked down. Monday blues?"

"Weird day. It's felt like everyone was watching me."

"First sign of paranoia. Next thing I'll be visiting you on the locked ward at the hospital."

"Yeah. I'll –"

Taylor's gaze jumped over her shoulder and widened. Rick, who'd been working beside her, joined them, gave Taylor a puzzled look and followed his gaze. "Whatcha lookin' at?" He grinned.

Sid turned. Through the glass partition, they could see the pottery workshop. Maria Morales was sitting at the electric potter's wheel, oblivious to everything as she coaxed a lump of clay into a symmetrical cone. She leaned forward slightly as she worked and her scoop-necked top revealed a generous amount of cleavage.

Rick sighed. "She could do that to me anytime." He looked ready to start drooling. "Reminds me of that old movie, *Ghost.* Ever see it? I think I was twelve when the babysitter brought that flick with her. I still remember the scene where the woman is doing that pottery thing and her ghost husband sits down behind her and starts caressing her hands and arms. And they're both slick with clay and..." He released a long slow breath.

"Hot," Taylor said in a matter-of-fact way.

"Oh, yeah."

Sid shook her head. Usually the person working the potter's wheel wore a smock to keep clean. "She's playing you. She knows that almost every guy in the place is watching her."

Rick released another breath. Taylor stared, unblinking.

Someone nudged Sid's back. She glanced to see Wes Remichuk, star basketball player and one of the jock set, smirking at her. "Maybe she's trying to get your attention, Sidney."

Sid's stomach twisted. "What do you mean?"

He peered down his nose at her. "Like you don't know."

Sid faced him, arms akimbo. "No, I don't. Explain it, *Wesley.*"

One eye twitched. "Everyone from the party knows what happened. Picked Joanne and dumped her on the same day. That's harsh."

"I didn't pick –"

rimshot on a high-pitched snare

"Though I can see why you dumped her. Next time go for someone at least a little cool." His gaze flicked down and back up. "Not that you're much better. Raving dyke."

Sid poked him in the chest. "I am not."

"Right. Like you weren't just ogling Maria along with the rest of us."

All Devin's lessons on how to take down an enemy rushed into Sid's mind. She clenched her fist but resisted to urge to plow Wes. "Commenting on the obvious isn't ogling."

Wes sneered. "Your friends might be too afraid to say anything – ever notice all your friends are guys? – but you're so butch it hurts. Admit it. Confession's supposed to be good for the soul."

"Yeah? How do you like this confession?" Sid caught him with a right hook to the underside of the jaw that staggered him back two steps.

Wes shook his head and came at her with fists raised.

"Don't move!" Mr. Franklin bellowed. Sid and Wes glared at each other but obeyed. The shop teacher inserted his lanky form between them. "Remichuk and Crowley, get to the office. I don't even want to know what this was about. You can explain it to VP Finning. And Taylor Janzen, get out of my class." He marched off, red-faced and muttering. They both stared after him. He spun and shouted, "Move! Now!" He reached for the phone on his desk and pointed toward the door.

Taylor grabbed Sid's arm and steered her out of the shop. "You haven't hit someone like that since you beat me up in grade four."

"You beat me up first." Sid yanked her arm free and stalked down the hall.

Footsteps followed but she didn't look. She'd been right about being watched all day – it had been the jock set, part of the inner circle of cool. Was the band having the same thoughts as Wes? Her fists were clenched when she walked into the office with Wes three steps behind her.

The secretary frowned at them. "Mr. Franklin called ahead. VP Finning is waiting." She used her pen to point at an open door behind her.

Sid took the seat nearest the door and made Wes step over her outstretched legs. She linked her fingers on her stomach, hoping she appeared calmer than she felt. *Jock set? Jerk set.*

The VP's expression was probably supposed to be firm, but her loose jowls just made her look like a bulldog with gas. Sid lowered her head to hide a smirk. The VP's tone, however, was harsh. After a staccato lecture, she said, "Ms. Crowley, the school has very strict rules about hitting. It's your first offence so you'll only be suspended for two days. Mr. Remichuk, if you were in any way an instigator in this incident, you will receive a one-day suspension. Now, who is going to tell me what happened?"

A silver analog clock ticked on the wall to their left. A fly buzzed in the window. The light from the window threw the VP's face into shadow, except for the whites of her eyes, which appeared brighter than normal. Alien. Sid looked down at her hands again and started tapping a beat with one index finger. This sucked on so many levels.

"Ms. Crowley," the VP finally said, "you can start. Why did you hit Mr. Remichuk?" Sid shrugged. She wasn't going to say anything that might get Wes suspended for a day. The VP sighed. "Mr. Remichuk?"

"I called her butch. She hit me."

He said it in such a cocky way Sid wanted to hit him again. Her finger tapped a faster rhythm. Again the clock and fly filled the silence. Finally the VP spoke again.

"Gender identity issues are not fodder for mocking or teasing, Mr. Remichuk. You'll be suspended for one day. Report to me on Wednesday morning. You are dismissed."

Wes stepped over Sid's legs just as she was bending them. He almost tripped, gave her a dark look and left the office. Sid braced her hands on the arms of the chair and started to push up.

"Ms. Crowley, I did not dismiss you." Sid sank back down with a sigh. The VP picked up her phone and spoke to someone, asking if they had a moment. She dropped the handset in its cradle and folded her hands together. "The counsellor will see you now."

Sid rose. "I don't need to see any counsellor. I'm going home."

Her hand was on the knob when the VP said, "Walk out of this school and you will be suspended for the week."

Sid dropped her hand. "Fine. I'm going to the counsellor's office. Okay?"

"Good. But I am making note of your attitude, Ms. Crowley. When you return on Thursday –" She opened a file folder and skimmed the contents. "Bring your father with you."

Minutes later Sid was sitting across the desk from the school counsellor, a twenty-something guy with collar-length, wavy blond hair and dark-rimmed, rectangular glasses. He wore his shirt untucked over beige jeans – maybe it was how he normally dressed but it made Sid feel like he was trying to win over the students. A laid back Mr. Casual whom you could trust with all your secrets.

He scooted his wheeled chair out from behind the desk and parked beside it, closer to Sid. He smiled. "We haven't met. I'm Mr. Brock, but you can call me Paul."

Sid blinked at this obvious "trust me" ploy. She said nothing.

A secretary stepped in and handed him a file. Sid could see her name. He didn't open it. "Tell me why VP Finning sent you here, Sidney."

"I'd rather go home and start serving my two-day suspension."

"I'm sure you would." He leaned back and gave her a little smile.

Sid looked around. The wall to her right, behind Brock's head, was a wall-to-wall bookcase, full except for a space in the centre of the middle shelf where a small TV-DVD combo player sat. Some DVDs were stacked beside it. Beside the window an inspirational poster urged you to strive for your dreams. On the wall to her left, another poster declared that you are special just the way you are. *Unless the way you are gets you into trouble,* Sid thought.

Three minutes passed with Sid looking at everything except Mr. Brock. She felt a twinge of victory when he finally opened the file. Sid got up and went over to the bookshelf. She wasn't much of a reader unless it was about drumming, but she ran her fingers over the spines and read titles just to pass the time. The DVDs were National Geographic specials.

Another few minutes passed before Mr. Brock said, "Please sit down, Sidney."

She pushed the chair farther away from him and sat.

"You resent being here."

This guy was quick. There'd be no fooling him. Sid shrugged.

"It seems, Sidney, that you were pretty fast to resort to violence."

"A jerk called me a name." She paused, searching for a pop psychology phrase that danced on the edge of her thoughts. "He invaded my personal space. I moved him out of it."

"By punching him in the jaw?"

"It worked."

"It's not likely, but he could lay charges. Why were you so quick to strike out?"

Sid cringed inwardly. Any moment she expected him to start talking about *anger issues.* This school was giving her anger issues. She'd been fine before today. She was done with this. Sid crossed her arms and started tapping a paradiddle rhythm against her ribs.

Mr. Brock droned on, trying to cajole her into talking.

Sid blinked when he said something about Dragonforce. She peered at him curiously.

"Glad you've decided to rejoin me." He pointed at Sid's black T-shirt. "I asked if you like Dragonforce."

Sid stared. Why would she wear their T-shirt if she didn't like them? Mr. Brock smiled in a mysterious way, like that Mona Lisa painting. "Dumb question, right? I used to listen to them, but metal isn't my thing anymore. What about them do you like? The lyrics?"

Sid considered whether this might be a trick question. After all, some metal lyrics could be considered a little, well, angry. His face remained open and curious, so she said, "Dave Mackintosh."

"It's been a while. What's his role again?"

"Drummer."

"Right." He paused. "Do you drum?"

Sid nodded at the same moment that the bell rang to end classes.

Mr. Brock took off his glasses. "Nothing like being saved by the bell, right Sidney?"

Instead of agreeing, she moved toward the door.

"I'll see you when you get back from your suspension."

"What?" Sid burst out.

Mr. Brock just smiled that annoying smile. "Thursday. Same time. I'll arrange with Mr. Franklin to release you from class."

Sid slammed the door.

4 | grooves in the arsenal

Halfway through Sid's two-day suspension and it felt like four. Her dad had left her a long list of spring cleaning chores to do while she was home. She couldn't get them done in triple the time. And James still expected her to go to her math tutor tonight, just like every Tuesday. What good was a suspension if it didn't get her out of doing math?

The worst part had been sitting down with James on Monday after supper and explaining it to him. Now he was worried she might have *violent tendencies.* Among other things.

"This is all my fault," James had said with a groan.

"How can it be your fault?" she'd asked.

"I never remarried."

"But you told me once that you never actually got a divorce."

"If I'd worked harder to have a female influence in your life, this wouldn't have happened. I thought Kathy living close by would be enough, but you hardly see your aunt or your cousins. You've grown up with only Devin and me. How were you supposed to learn to be a girl?"

"Dad," she'd replied. "I am a girl."

"Well, yes, but you don't act like one, do you?"

What, Sid wondered, had happened to women's liberation and being able to do what you wanted? Shortly after their talk, Devin had called from college, asking for Sid. She was sure James had set it up. So she had told Devin what had happened. He had snickered and said, "That's my sis." His being cool about it had at least helped Sid try to shrug it off.

All Monday night James had popped antacid tablets like crazy. He'd tried to be sneaky, but Sid had noticed. She was worried about him; he was worried about her. What a freaking mess.

Sid was cleaning yet another window – how could a smallish house have so many windows? – when the phone rang. She answered with a brusque, "Crowley's."

"Sid?"

"Yeah..." She drew it out. The voice was vaguely familiar but she couldn't place it.

"Tim Rocklin here." Sid's breath caught. The Fourth Down's bass player. He continued, "We're jamming at my place and are trying out a few guys on drums. Someone said you're pretty good and want to play. Thought you might like to come over. Audition, like."

"I'd love to. Ah, when?"

"Another guy's trying out in about two minutes. Give us forty."

Sid bit the inside of her lip and thought furiously. It was five o'clock and tutoring wasn't until half past seven. James was working late again and might not make it home before that.

Rocklin cleared his throat. "Sound good?"

James wouldn't even know she'd slipped out. "Yeah. I'll be there."

"Great." He hung up.

Sid hit the off button and punched the air, phone in hand. "My break! Woohoo!" She danced around the living room, then stopped. Crap. She didn't know Rocklin's address. She phoned Taylor, barely letting him say hello. "Tell me you know where Tim Rocklin lives."

"Sure. Other side of the school, in one of those rich cul-de-sacs near the ravine. Why?"

"I have to be there in forty minutes."

"Aren't you, like, grounded until the suspension ends?"

"Don't quibble, Tay. This is my chance. I'm auditioning. Can you give me a ride?"

"What if Mr. J finds out?"

"He won't unless you tell him."

Taylor sighed, then agreed, reluctance dripping from every word. Thirty-five minutes later he deposited her in the driveway of a house triple the size of her bungalow. He waved and headed off to gas up. His motorbike's roar echoed off the semicircle of what James would call executive homes. Sid practically hugged the box containing her kick pedal as she rang the doorbell. Nervous, yes, but totally pumped.

Someone in an apron answered the door, giving Sid a

cursory, disapproving glance. *Maybe I should've changed out of my grungy housecleaning clothes.* The woman opened the door wider. "You must be the other young man Timothy said would be coming. They're in the basement. This way." Her rubber-soled shoes barely whispered on the tiled floor. Hired help, Sid realized.

She descended the staircase the woman indicated, heading toward the sound of laughter and found the band sprawled in some home-theatre chairs drinking beer. Tim Rocklin, called Rock by his friends, spotted her and raised his bottle. "Want a beer before you start, Sid?"

"No, thanks. I prefer playing clean."

He curled his top lip. "You know the guys?"

Everyone knew Jeff Clementine (Clem) and Han Walser. Both good athletes and better musicians. Han nodded; Clem stared. Sid fought the urge to shuffle. She refused to look nervous even if her heart was rattling a rapid snare drum tattoo.

Han indicated the box Sid clutched tightly. "Whatcha got there?"

"My kick pedal." A look of approval crossed his face.

Rocklin said, "You're Devin's sister. You play as good as him?"

"He's lead guitar so it's hard to compare. I'm as good as any drummer his band had."

"We'll judge that. Let's do it."

She trailed them into the next room where Rocklin had a complete band set-up. He even had some basic recording equipment. The drum kit was better than hers – nothing second-hand for Rocklin – but as soon as she tried these she decided her own cymbals had better tone. It took her a few minutes to attach her pedal, wishing it was the cooler double kick pedal. *Someday.* Then she adjusted and positioned the throne. The rest would have to wait until she was a member of the band.

They kept to easy songs from a drummer's point of view. Basic rock grooves. She was able to add a few fills, spice it up a little. Han switched between lead guitar and keyboards, depending on the song. Clem played a solid lead guitar. Rocklin was awesome on bass, which was surprising considering how big he was, fingers included. But they flew, as fast and delicate as hummingbirds.

The tempo picked up as the session progressed. They were halfway through a song when Rocklin turned and yelled over the music, "Let's see you solo, Sid. In place of the chorus."

Sid nodded. She'd hoped they'd want this. She'd been developing a solo almost for as long as she'd been playing. She gave them the full meal deal. Drummed her heart out. She felt the rhythm thrumming through her and knew she'd nailed it, ending it with a double hit – ride and crash cymbals together – that was her version of ending with a gong like Neil Peart did.

The cymbal vibrations faded away into silence. Sid laid the sticks on the snare drum and waited, the mantra of "Let me be your drummer" chanting through her mind.

Finally, Rocklin said, "That was decent." Sid suppressed a

smile but inside she was grinning. He asked, "You covered a lot of ground. Anything you can't do?"

"I still can't do double hand crossovers. I'm working on it."

Rocklin nodded. Clem said, "We don't do drum solos in our gig." He started to say something else, glanced at Rocklin and pressed his lips into a sneer.

Sid almost asked why they bothered listening to hers, then decided it was the best way to show them what she had. She loved soloing, but said, "I can live with that. I just want to play."

Rocklin nodded again. "We all like to do that. We'll have to talk about it, Sid. You know we tried out another guy. Maybe you know him: Wes Remichuk?"

Sid blinked. "I didn't know he drummed."

"He picked up sticks about a year ago. He's okay."

Sid had been playing for over three years, had taken lessons on and off, and knew without hearing him that she was better than Wes. "Whatever you decide." She'd said it cool, just like Devin would. Inside, her grin had widened to a maniacal width.

After Sid got her kick pedal back in its box, Clem said, "Are you going to tell her or not, Rock?" His outburst earned him a silencing look, which he ignored. "You're the one who's always saying we've got to be out front with each other, that bands fall apart when the members start pissing around."

"Tell me what?" Sid asked. The inner grin had evaporated.

Clem slammed down the lid of his guitar case and snapped the catches closed. He turned to face her, his expression stony. "I don't want a chick in the band."

"We've been through this, Clem," Rocklin said. "We decided –"

"No," Clem replied. "You decided. Maybe if she'd hooked up with Joanne it'd be okay."

Sid looked from Clem to Rocklin, trying to decipher what the issue was. Rocklin shrugged in her direction. "Clem figures guys will fight over a chick if she's in the band. But that isn't likely to happen in this case, even if you aren't gay." His gaze ran over Sid and she felt judgment in his suddenly closed expression.

Wearing her work clothes had definitely been a mistake. Sid's stomach squeezed as she felt her chance slipping away. She wasn't sure she should say anything but what did it matter at this point? "So, Clem only wants me to play if I'm into chicks and you'll only take me if I look better? What does Han think?"

Han, who'd been leaning against the wall listening, avoided her gaze.

Clem's tone was irritated. "Han always votes with Rock."

"Which means what?"

Rock replied, "You impressed us enough today that we might let you play a gig with us to see how it goes. But... we're style-setters, Crowley, not refugees. You want to play with us you'd better clean up. We take our music seriously but we also look good on stage." He gave her the once-over again and shook his head.

In her mind, Sid heard the drumbeat of a death march as her hopes were flung under a guillotine.

5 | accent on the upbeats

Here it was, Wednesday night, and Sid admitted she was not looking forward to going back to school tomorrow. She still hadn't heard from Rocklin about that possible gig. If she didn't make it into The Fourth Down she was going to scream. Then there was Wes. Bad enough she'd hit him. If she did beat him out, he might try to rouse the wrath of the jock set. They stuck together tighter than a hillbilly clan. If she had the stamp of approval from TFD, she should be safe, but you never knew what would set them off.

With her earphones in and her iPod on half volume, Sid tried to keep her mind occupied by learning a new song. She'd found the drum tabs on the Internet, but even with that it was proving tricky. She was going through the song for the nine or tenth time when Taylor and Narain bounded down the stairs. Taylor's foot slid off the last step and he staggered sideways, stopping before he bumbled into the TV stand.

Sid tugged her earphones free. "My jailer is letting me have visitors?"

Taylor sprawled onto the carpet near the sofa, as if the floor were the safest place for him. "Yup. But Mr. J said we can't stay long."

Narain plopped onto one end of the sofa and picked up a *Drum* magazine Sid had left on the end table. He fanned the pages. "There's to be no physical contact between the prisoner and visitors. He assured us all visits are being monitored. Maybe he got wind of your jailbreak last night." He dropped the magazine. "What were you playing? It sounded pretty tame."

Sid left her sticks and iPod on the throne and claimed the other end of the sofa. "A jazz piece."

Narain's brown eyes grew round. "Jazz?"

Taylor laughed. "Now you know our metal queen's secret, Narain. She also likes jazz. Weird, huh? She says it has influenced metal but she's not gonna convince me of that. I'm happier thinking she has a split personality."

"And I like Rush. They aren't metal. It's all about the drumming." Sid sniffed and decided to change the topic. "Did you eat at your grandmother's tonight, Narain?"

He scowled. "What makes you think so?"

"Every time you do, you smell like a jumble of spices. What's that one they use so much in East Indian cooking?"

"Cumin," he muttered.

"Yeah. That's what you smell like."

"I had no choice. It was my grandfather's birthday. I'd rather have eaten at a pizza joint."

Sid tapped his shin with her toe. "I'm not hassling you

about it. Dad took Devin and me to an East Indian restaurant once. It was good. Well, except for one dish. The waitress warned us it was hot, but Dad said to try it. I think my mouth burned for two days."

Narain smiled. She liked making him smile, liked the way his teeth shone white against his brown skin.

Taylor slapped the rug. "Now that we've covered music and food, let's get to the important stuff. What happened with the audition? You were gone when I swung by Rocklin's to pick you up."

"I walked home. Needed to unwind." Sid's gaze bounced between her friends. "No word around school yet?" They both shook their heads. She told them the story, but couldn't bring herself to quote Rocklin about her looking like a refugee. That had stung and she knew Taylor would howl over it.

Apprehension etched Taylor's brow. "Wait a minute. You hit Wes because he called you butch, but you didn't tell the band you aren't?"

"Yeah, well, I overreacted with Wes. His attitude pisses me off."

"You're not into lying, Sid. Why would you lie about that?" Taylor's eyebrows had scrunched together as he spoke.

"Clem will go on a full out campaign against me as soon as I admit it. I didn't lie. I just didn't set them straight. That's all."

Narain said, "That's *not* all, Sid. Wes might be your bigger problem. He got suspended for a day because of you. And if you beat him out to be TFD's drummer, he might be ticked enough to turn the jock set against you." Sid nodded at the echo of her earlier thoughts.

Taylor said, "You're one of 'em, Narain. You'll be able to warn us if that happens."

"He isn't one of them," Sid said and turned to Narain. "I mean, you play sports, but you don't have that own-the-hallways attitude."

Narain's shoulders twitched. "Bottom line." He leaned forward. "If they decide to make your days miserable, it'll happen."

"Why would they do that?"

"Because they can."

"What wonderful logic."

Taylor said, "Maybe you should hope that Wes gets into TFD. At least then he'd be too busy to be gunning for you."

"No way. I'm better than he is. I deserve that gig."

Taylor's expression darkened. "And you'll lie to get it."

Sid kicked the air in his direction. "Give it a rest, Tay. As soon as I do that practise gig with them they'll realize how good I am and Clem won't care that I'm not gay. I'll clear it up then. It doesn't mean anything."

"Sure. So are you gonna hook up with a girl just to keep up appearances?"

"Don't be a jerk."

Narain cleared his throat. "Cool it, you two. I don't want to have to call the warden." His eyebrows jigged toward the ceiling. He stuffed his hands into his jeans pockets. Designer jeans.

Sid felt the need to come clean. "There's one way Wes has me beat."

"He's a better liar?" Taylor asked.

She scowled at him. "No, he's a better dresser."

Narain smiled. "No offence, Sid, but that doesn't take much. Though I see your point. The guys in TFD like their labels. Too bad you don't have a mom around to give you advice." He gave her a compassionate glance. She rolled her eyes. That was ancient history.

Taylor said, "She dresses like Devin. He was cool."

Sid thought about the disdainful look Rocklin had given her clothes. "Devin doesn't need to have style. He has talent."

"You have talent, Sid. You don't need cool clothes any more than you need lies." Taylor arched his eyebrows.

Sid's breath escaped in a hiss. Did he have to keep needling her? Didn't he realize how important this was? Besides, he was so wrong. She wasn't going to pretend she was gay just for Clem, so she needed clothes. Cool clothes. She ignored the barb. "So... No great ideas?"

Taylor's expression said, "Don't look at me." He rolled onto his stomach and picked at the red shag threads. Narain avoided her gaze and looked up at the tile ceiling.

What a useless pair of friends, Sid thought. *How do I reinvent myself?*

6 | two beat fill

Flying under the jock set's radar was hard work. Sid had made James take her to school early, before the students usually started arriving, so he could assure VP Finning he had talked to Sid about the seriousness of her situation. She'd had to duck low a few times as some track-and-field jocks had jogged past the office after early practise – she'd forgotten their coach was an early riser kind of guy.

All day she'd kept her head down and kept moving. Hard to hit a moving target. But she'd kept her ears open and there was still no word if TFD had chosen a drummer. The suspense left her stomach gnarled and rebelling at the thought of food so she'd hidden in the library stacks during lunch. That's when she'd run across the psychology section and had thumbed through a few books. Now she knew how she was going to handle Mr. Brock.

The day had gone well, until she walked into shop class and saw Wes Remichuk sitting on a stool beside her work space. She ignored him as long as she could, getting out the chest she was almost finished, some brushes and varnish, laying out a tarp, finding a screwdriver to pry open the can and a stick to stir the varnish. Finally, she stopped moving.

She felt like a bull's-eye was painted on her forehead. *Be cool,* she told herself. *Like playing ghost notes.* After all, no word from TFD meant he was edgy, too.

Wes said, "Hear you been ducking out of sight all day. Hiding from me?"

"Not hiding. I'm busy. Prepping for my visit with Mr. Brock." No point hiding anything about that when Mr. Franklin was going to call her out of class at any moment.

Wes leaned forward. "Going to shrink your brain, is he?"

"At least I have something for him to shrink." Sid bit the inside of her lip – that was more like hitting the crash cymbal than playing a ghost note. Stupid.

"A real smart-ass, aren't you?"

She was fighting the temptation to reply when her woodworking neighbour, Rick, tapped Wes's shoulder. "You're in my way, Wes. Your assigned space is over there." His thumb pointed over his shoulder. "Say... Nice bruise on your jaw." His voice dropped to a conspiratorial whisper. "But there's a wicked rumour going around that you got beat up by a girl."

Sid started laughing. She couldn't help it. The dirty look Wes gave her set off a drum roll in her head, but she didn't care. Wes stomped off. Rick gave her a wink and whispered, "Remind me to never get you mad, Sid. Your right hook is awesome. Where'd you learn it?"

"My brother. Taylor was the first person I tried it on. You

should ask him about it."

Rick chuckled.

From his desk, Mr. Franklin called out, "Class has started, people."

Sid opened the varnish and got to work on the bridal chest. It wasn't big, the size of two bread boxes, so she only had the back panel left to varnish when Mr. Franklin told her it was time to go to the office. Rick asked if he could finish her first coat so she could apply the whole second coat tomorrow. Mr. Franklin gave Rick's lopsided shelf a skeptical look but agreed.

"Thanks, Rick."

"No problem. I'll clean up for you, too. It's not like I'm making any progress on my shelf."

"Maybe I can help you square it off."

"Great. Better go. Franklin's giving you the evil eye."

Minutes later, she stood before the counsellor's door, a little nervous at the thought of putting her plan into action. She smoothed her white T-shirt. It had been a careful choice this morning – nothing dark and metal that might suggest violence or anger, just the cool Starman that was Rush's logo. Behind her, the secretary encouraged her to knock.

She raised her hand the same instant that Mr. Brock opened the door. "Hi, Sidney. I saw you walk into the general office." He indicated the window beside the door that allowed the secretary to see into his office. "I thought maybe you had decided to sneak out through the staff room." He indicated the other direction.

"No. I'm here for my medicine."

"Since I'm not a psychiatrist, I can't prescribe any." He stepped aside and waved her in.

Same as Monday, he scuttled his chair sideways like a crab until he was beside the desk and closer to Sid. Today he wore a patterned green shirt and darker green jeans. He looked very relaxed as he leaned back in his chair and rocked it slightly. Sid wished she were half so calm. It felt like someone was rapidly tapping a ride cymbal in her stomach.

Brock smiled. "Nice Rush T-shirt. Do you like this band for its drummer, too?"

Sid wanted to say what she'd planned then get out. She gave a terse nod.

"Who is it?"

Didn't this man know anything about music? Sid's breath huffed out. "Neil Peart. He writes a lot of their lyrics, too."

"He's good?"

"One of the best." Sid was still tense but was trying not to show it. The sooner they moved past this friendly chat, the better.

Brock did move. He asked her how she'd spent her two days off school, so she told him how she'd been her dad's house elf and how he'd lectured her, a lot, on the importance of getting an education and all that jazz. Which wasn't completely true. He'd mentioned it in passing during their talk on Monday evening, but every time he'd popped another antacid tablet it had felt like a lecture. The whole time, Brock nodded like a bobble-head, apparently pleased with her remorse.

Then came the moment she'd prepped for. "Let's talk about hitting Wesley."

"I've thought about it a lot, Mr. Brock-"

"Paul. You're supposed to call me Paul."

She blinked. "I know you think I'm angry. I'm not. Really. I think I'm confused."

"Oh? So when you're confused you hit people?"

"No. That was, well, maybe it was a flash of anger. But mostly it was just me being confused." She pointed at her file, which Brock had left on his desk. "You have to know I don't have a mom. Something Dad said on Monday made me realize that's why I hit Wes."

"You have a mother, Sydney, she just isn't part of your household."

"No, I really don't have a mom. She did more than left us. She *resigned.* When she left she told Dad she didn't want anything to do with being a wife or mom. And she never has, not in the twelve years since she walked out." Sid willed Brock to take the bait. Sure she'd been upset about her mother leaving...twelve years ago. She had a single memory of being tiny and her dad rocking her while she kicked and wailed that she wanted her mommy.

"Where is she now?"

"Don't know. I think Dad keeps track, but I've never asked."

Head down, Sid watched Brock from the corner of her eye. She was dumping all this too fast, she decided. She needed to slow down, let him coax stuff from her. More important, she needed to loosen the band squeezing her chest. Taylor was right: lying wasn't her style.

Brock leaned forward and rested his forearms on his knees. "So having no mother on the scene makes you angry?"

"Not angry," she whispered. "Confused. Devin and Dad are great. They taught me lots of stuff, but it was all guy stuff. I don't know how girls handle being insulted. In the movies, they cry, but I'm sure not going to do that. Guys hit. So that's what I did to Wes."

She kept her hands clasped so she wasn't tempted to start tapping out a rhythm. Was he going to bite? Was he going to let her blame everything on someone she hadn't thought about in years? Someone she hadn't cared about for pretty much as long as she could remember.

The bobble started again, barely noticeable but there. Sid's breath huffed out in relief. But her body didn't relax – her stomach still quivered, her calves felt on the verge of cramping.

"You've obviously given this a lot of thought, Sidney, and I think you are possibly right. But have you given any thought to what you're going to do about it? Going around hitting people isn't a useful approach to conflict resolution. Quite the opposite."

"I think... I need to learn to be a girl." *Reinvent myself.*

"How are you going to do that?"

"I have an idea or two, but I'm not totally sure."

Brock pointed at the poster on the wall, the one about being special just as you are. "Trying to figure out who you are is a good thing. Just remember that you have a lot of good qualities already. Girls don't fit a single mould any more than guys do."

Which showed how little Brock knew about high school. If you didn't fit in one of the accepted moulds, you were a freak, or an outcast, or both. And at this point, if she didn't get into The Fourth Down she was as good as socially out-cast. The audition had gotten their attention but she had to keep it. Their approval could erase the target Wes was trying to paint on her back.

Brock laid a hand on the arm of Sid's chair. "Peer pressure can be a powerful force, Sidney. Don't sacrifice too much just to fit in, okay?" She didn't reply – it was like he'd been reading her mind and it was freaky. He leaned back and asked, "Out of curiosity, how much would you give up? Would you stop drumming?"

Sid jerked her head up. He was so off; this was all about drumming. Her one heel began to jitter. "No. I wouldn't give it up for anything. I'm not...selling my soul here. I'm only trying to figure out who I am."

To her surprise, Brock nodded at the corny statement. "Okay. That's righteous." Sid almost rolled her eyes – who ever, anywhere, said *righteous?* He added, "I want to see you again to touch base and see how you're handling things."

She fought to keep her face neutral. This was not part of the plan. She had done the confessional thing so she wouldn't have to come back.

"So long as nothing else comes up, why don't you come

back next Thursday, okay?" Brock took off his glasses and gave her that "trust me" smile.

Sid nodded and escaped. She almost ran to her locker, grabbed her books, stuffed them in her backpack and shot to the nearest exit. She needed fresh air before the smell of this place made her puke. Wax and metal and disinfectant and bodies. Too many bodies. All with eyes – eyes that watched too much, accused too much, judged too much. Why couldn't Brock back off?

She was half a block from the school when the last bell rang. She walked as fast as she could without breaking into a run. Her heart pounded like a double bass beat.

What was wrong with her? What had happened to staying cool? This wasn't part of the plan. She'd handed Brock her "woe is me, my mother abandoned me" line. And he'd eaten it like it was a plate of warm chocolate chip cookies.

Sid started to run. Someone drove by and honked. She didn't look. And she didn't stop until she turned onto her street. Six blocks. She wheezed and pressed her hand against her ribs, and wondered if this reinvention project should include some fitness training. No way. Not if it meant she'd have to get near any of the jock set.

Footsteps pounded behind her. There was no flight left in her, so she dropped her backpack and spun, ready to fight. Taylor stumbled toward her.

"Didn't you hear me, Sid?" He bent over and gasped in big mouthfuls of air. After a moment, he straightened. "I've been trying to catch you since I left school. What's wrong?"

Sid snatched up her pack and started walking. Taylor caught up and nudged her shoulder. "Did the counsellor piss you off?"

Just the mention of the word counsellor made her muscles notch tighter. "Leave it, Tay. I just want to let loose."

"Yup. He pissed you off. So what're you gonna do? Beat up your drums?"

"No. Right now I feel like I'd break something. I can't afford to start replacing drums."

"Wow. What *did* he say?"

"I don't want to talk, Tay. I need..." Sid paused as a thought struck her. "Would you take me for a ride on your bike? That ride last Saturday was great. We could find some paved side roads, open it up. Get this stink out of my head."

They arrived at Taylor's driveway. "Stink, huh? Sure. Mom had early shift so she'll be home by now. Let me tell her where we're going." He took Sid's backpack and left her standing on the concrete.

Sid didn't have to tell anyone where she was. Devin was at college; James was at work and wouldn't be home until at least 6:30. What was it like, she wondered, to have someone waiting for you after school, someone who wanted to know how your day was and who nagged you to do homework?

Sid scowled at Taylor's front door. For twelve years she'd gotten along fine with only Devin and James. What did she need a mother for? Bad enough when James hassled her about stuff without having another adult adding to the chorus.

Why did she think it was a good idea to feed that abandoned waif junk to Brock? She wished that he was a jerk. It might be easier to lie to someone she didn't sort of like.

7 | reverse quadruplet

The bike ride and some drumming had scrubbed Sid's thoughts clean. She was back on track with her plan. And Devin's cheerful voice was the perfect end to a good practise session. "Hey, little sis. Things looking up?"

"Yeah." Before he could ask anything else, Sid said, "Did I tell you that Taylor and his dad finally got his motorbike running?"

"No kidding? Didn't think that would ever happen."

"And what's totally weird is that he isn't clumsy when he's driving it."

Devin snorted. "Maybe he just needed to get off his feet."

Sid chuckled. "Yeah. You could be right. Do you think Dad would let me get –"

"No way."

"Why not?"

"Because he never let me get one. Don't you think I asked?" Someone said something to Devin in the background. He said, "Sounds like my roommate is trashing the apartment, looking for his calculator or something. Gotta run. I'll be home for the wedding if we don't talk sooner."

"So stay in touch, text or Facebook me. Use the technology."

"I'll try. I'm really busy. Spring session is crammed. 'Bye."

The connection went dead. Sid hit the "end" button. She hated not having Devin around. All the other college students she knew were back home working for the summer, but he wanted to do four years of study in three, so wouldn't be home until the end of June.

Her cousin's wedding was in ten days. She didn't much like fancy parties, and it would be fancy if Aunt Kathy was planning it, but at least she'd see Devin. But now she had to phone Aunt Kathy's and talk to her dear, sweet cousin, Heather. *Gag,* Sid thought, as she dialed the number. If Heather didn't agree to help her, the next part of the plan was going to be tricky.

Aunt Kathy answered and it took a minute for Heather to pick up the phone. The surprise in her voice was evident. And she didn't mince words. "Sidney, you never call me. What's up?"

"I... Well, Heath, I have –"

"Heather. Not Heath."

"Right. Heather. I have a problem. What you might call a...fashion emergency."

Silence. Five seconds. Ten. Then, "You aren't a fashion emergency, Sidney. You're a fashion disaster and have been for years."

Ouch. Sid bit back a snide retort and said, "Yeah. That's why I need your help."

"Why?"

Sid heard the suspicion and couldn't blame Heather for it. "Because you know about fashion and I want, I mean, *need* to learn."

More silence. Sid was expecting Heather to hang up when she said, "We might be able to help each other. If you're serious."

"Yeah. Totally serious. But what do you need help with?"

"I'll come over and tell you then." She hung up.

Sid couldn't believe how nervous she was when Heather rang the doorbell fifteen minutes later. From his office, James yelled, "Who's at the door, Sid?"

"It's Heather," she replied.

"Hi, Uncle James," Heather chimed.

James appeared in his office doorway. "Heather? Ah, nice to see you. What brings you over?"

She smiled sweetly. She was good at sweet. "Fashion consultation."

James's mouth opened but no words came out. Sid said, "No sweat, Dad. I'll fill you in later. Downstairs or my room, Heather?"

"Your room, of course. We have to see what's in your closet."

They walked past James. He was still gaping. Sid could feel his gaze until she closed her door. Heather dropped her purse on Sid's black comforter, sat on the edge of the bed and scanned the room with her nose wrinkled. "Rock band posters.

What a surprise. Do I even want to look in your closet?"

Sid bounced onto the bed, earning an irritated glance. Heather patted her hair. It was perfect, obviously styled with care, and dyed a shade blonder than it would normally be, Sid suspected. Makeup and jewelry and layered tops over jeans that looked pressed. Who ironed jeans? And her flat polka-dot shoes matched the bottom shirt or camisole or whatever it was. All this just to visit your cousin who didn't care about fashion?

Who was Sid kidding? She was way out of her depth here. She cleared her throat. "Why are you so eager to help if you know what a disaster I am?"

"It's a challenge." At Sid's skeptical look, Heather tapped her teeth with a polished nail. "And I had to get out of that house. I mean, I like fashion. I like decorating. But the closer the wedding gets, the crazier Mom and Mandi get. Everything's perfect, but they agonize over every detail. Mandi is like, like a mother bear with PMS who's suffering caffeine withdrawal."

Sid laughed. She stopped when she saw that Heather was serious. Her eyes were even shining with tears. "So they're stressing you out. How will trying to help me help you?"

"I really don't have anything I can help them with now that the table favours are done and the silk flower arrangements are made. I have to help out on the weekend of the wedding, of course, but until then, the more I'm out of that house, the better. Really. That circus could turn a girl off getting married altogether. Dad has been muttering about the benefits of elopement for weeks and I'm starting to think he has a point."

Sid had forgotten how long-winded Heather's answers could be. They were the same age, but except for family gatherings they didn't see each other at all. Different schools, different interests, different everything.

Heather went to Sid's closet and flung open the doors with dramatic flair. She stood in silence for a moment, then closed the doors and leaned against them. "This is going to be worse than I thought. There are only band T-shirts hanging in there. You don't have a single dress. Not one top that could be considered at all feminine. I suppose your dresser drawers are full of jeans, a few pair of shorts, and a hideous bathing suit."

"You forgot to mention the underwear and socks and PJ bottoms."

"You sleep topless?"

"I sleep with old T-shirts."

"Oh. Of course." Heather straightened and brushed off her hands. She retrieved her purse and pulled out a green roll.

"What's that?"

"A tape measure. First we have to figure out your size. So. Shirt and jeans off."

Sid blinked. "You expect me to strip?"

"Do you want my help or not?"

"Can't we just measure with my clothes on?"

Heather stuck out her hip and planted her fist on it. "We do it my way, Sidney, or we don't do it." She didn't move.

Her aquamarine eyes were like lasers outlined by mascara.

Sid sighed. She'd wanted this. "And all these years I thought you were a wimp."

"Why? Because I can't break eardrums and build bookcases? Believe me, if you want to survive in the shadow of a prima donna older sister, you have to get tough."

"In a pretty and feminine kind of way."

Heather smiled. Sweetly. "Of course. Clothes off, cousin."

Sid muttered under her breath as she peeled off her jeans and top. She felt stupid. She crossed her arms and glared at Heather, who gave an exaggerated sigh.

"Arms out, Sidney, so I can measure. What is with the cotton panties and the sports bra?"

"They're comfortable."

"Maybe, but if you want me to teach you about fashion, you'll have to trust me."

"I don't like the sound of that. What does it have to do with my underwear?"

"Think lace, Sidney. Lace and bras that enhance instead of hide. We are going to have to dress you from the skin out." Heather stepped behind Sid and positioned the measuring tape.

"That's stupid." The tape was cold where it touched skin. Sid glanced down at the green strip that stretched across her breasts.

"Hm. Better than I expected," Heather said. "Those T-shirts are hiding actual curves."

"I'm not throwing them out."

"Wear them when you practise your drums. But if you want my help, you have to follow my instructions, and that means no band shirts and cargoes outside this house."

"You're harsh."

"You're desperate, or you wouldn't have called me."

While Heather measured Sid's hips and thighs, Sid stared at the Rush poster at the head of her bed and tried not to be embarrassed. Neil stared back, not offering any advice. Heather was right. She was desperate – enough that she was willing to try to reinvent herself. Heather was a lot smarter than she remembered.

Heather rolled up her tape measure. "Well, are we going to do it my way?"

Sid clenched her jaw for a few seconds, then closed her eyes. "Yeah."

"Good. We'll go on our first shopping trip tomorrow right after school."

"First?" squeaked Sid.

Heather smiled and waltzed across the room. "See you tomorrow." She closed the door behind her and Sid flopped onto the bed. Down the hall Heather practically sang, "Good night, Uncle James."

Sid groaned and laid her arm across her eyes.

"What's going on, Sid? Oh, geez –" James closed the door way louder than he'd opened it.

Torn between laughter and embarrassment, Sid scrambled for her T-shirt. "I'll be right out, Dad. We need to talk. I think I might need to borrow some money."

8 | sixteenth note variations

Taylor leaned against his bike. "What do you mean, you can't hang out tonight? I thought we'd cruise around, get a pizza, see a movie."

That sounded worlds better than what her night was going to be like. Sid scuffed her toe against the concrete. "Can't. That's all. I have this family thing..."

"What family thing?"

"Um. Heather's...helping me shop for stuff. For the wedding." *Among other things,* Sid added silently.

"Heather? Your Barbie-doll cousin? That Heather?"

Sid nodded.

"You can't stand Heather."

"I know that. You think I don't know that? You think this is going to be fun? I know nothing about girl's clothes, Tay. I need help." She tugged at the hem of her T-shirt.

"You look fine."

"Yeah. That carries as much weight as Devin saying it. We're friends. You don't look at me like a girl any more than

I look at you like a guy."

Taylor narrowed his eyes. "Since when do you care what you look like? This has something to do with that band audition, doesn't it?"

"I need to get home. Heather'll be there any minute."

"Sid, don't hold out on me. What's up?"

"Nothing."

"Liar."

Sid opened her mouth and snapped it shut, spun away and headed home. When Taylor called for her to come back, she swatted her hand in his direction as if he were a fly, but didn't look back. The last thing she needed right now was to get grilled by her best friend. Why couldn't he simply trust her? She knew what she was doing. She had a plan.

She had just dropped her backpack by the front closet when she heard a vehicle pull into the driveway. She jogged into James's office and snatched up the envelope with her name on it. He had promised to get some cash and to drop it off during his lunch break.

When she thought about it, he had been incredibly cheerful about giving her shopping money. She opened the envelope and counted the cash. It was double what she had asked for. She blinked rapidly, wondering what that was supposed to mean. Was she way underestimating the cost of clothes or was he that eager for her to get some different stuff? Did he want her to look like Heather? Was he embarrassed by her?

Sid rolled the money into a wad and stuffed it in the front

pocket of her cargoes, hating that a vibrating cymbal had taken up residence in her stomach. She rushed out of the house and dove into the back seat of Aunt Kathy's bronze-coloured SUV.

Her aunt gave her a quick up-and-down glance. "Hi, honey. I haven't seen you in ages. It's so sweet that you and Heather are going shopping together."

Sid's smile was plastic. She nodded vaguely and looked out the window.

"Where's your purse, honey? Did you forget it?"

Sid returned her attention to the front seat where the middle-aged Barbie and the teen Barbie both stared at her with round eyes and earnest expressions. Sid frowned. "Don't own one. Can we go?"

Heather settled back in her seat. "Didn't I tell you, Mom? Fashion emergency."

Aunt Kathy tsked. "Don't be rude, Heather."

Sid pressed her forehead against the cool window. *But it's true,* she thought. As the SUV backed into the street, Sid desperately wished there was some other way to remake herself.

Humpty Dumpty had a great fall. *Yeah. Already did that.*

All the king's horses and all the king's men, couldn't put Humpty together again. *But Heather can. And she's so good at putting on makeup, no one will even see my scars.*

Fifteen minutes later they arrived at the Hall of Torture, otherwise known as West Towne Mall. As they headed to the main entrance Aunt Kathy called that she would pick them up at nine o'clock.

"Five hours?" Sid asked. "What are we going to do for five hours?"

"Shop, silly."

Sid groaned. A smirk flitted across Heather's lips. Sid said, "You're going to enjoy this, aren't you?"

"In so very many ways, cousin dear."

"If I weren't –"

"Desperate? But you are, remember?" Heather tossed her head in a smug way that made Sid want to trip her. How did she manage to toss her head and not look like a horse? It was annoying. But then everything about her cousin was annoying, especially her confidence.

By the end of two hours, Sid was pleading for a rest. They already had more bags than Sid thought they'd have by the end of the night. Who knew that bra and panty shopping could be so intense? Or that lingerie shops were so...shimmery? Or that "the basics" needed different accessories for each combination? Or that shoes could look so nice and be so uncomfortable? (Though she'd always suspected as much.)

Heather agreed to a supper break and they each bought a sandwich in the food court. Sid moaned happily as she took her first bite of her broiled Philly cheese steak special. She wiped a dribble of sauce from the corner of her mouth and said, "Why didn't you get a full-sized sub, Heather? Aren't you starving after all that walking?"

Heather picked up her turkey and veggie (hold the cheese) sandwich. "I like fitting into my jeans, thanks."

Sid took another huge bite and a swallow of cola. "I didn't

ask you for diet advice. You aren't going to make me start eating like a sick sparrow."

Issuing one of her dramatic sighs, Heather said, "Of course not. I'll work with what I've been given. That will be a big enough miracle for now."

Sid slammed down her cup. "I'm going to get very sick of you."

"Oh, you'll put up with me. Because a tiny part of you wants to look like I do."

"Don't flatter yourself. I'm doing this to survive. I was fine with how I looked."

A skeptical look landed on Heather's face. "What happened to change your mind?"

"Not your business." She was on the verge of telling Heather to stuff her shopping trip when she spotted a friend. "I'll be right back." She wended between the tables toward a familiar white afro and tapped a tweed shoulder. "Hi, Rake."

The man who looked up, dark brown skin weathered like old leather, could have been anywhere between 45 and 65. Sid had never been able to get him to tell, though she figured he was probably closer to the 65 end of things. He smiled broadly. "Sid! I haven't seen you in a good while. Where you been keeping yourself?"

"School, home practising my drums, not much else."

Rake tapped her T-shirt at her waist. "Look at this vile piece of clothing. You're still drumming that evil rock 'n roll, aren't you?" His eyes sparked and Sid couldn't help grinning.

"You know me."

"I do. I surely do. When are you gonna drop by the club again? We still jam every Sunday. We'd like you to stop by. Ten Pin's arthritis is acting up again. Getting harder for him to keep the beat."

"Soon, Rake. I promise. I've been practising."

"Jazz will win your soul, yet."

Sid laughed and picked up the fedora on the seat beside Rake. "Haven't I told you to keep this on your head? One of these days, I'm going to swipe this beauty from you."

He winked. "Thieving works better if you don't tell folks what you're planning."

Sid set the fedora on Rake's head and squeezed his shoulder. "I'll drop by the club soon."

"You're always welcome, hon."

Sid was smiling when she rejoined her cousin.

"Who was that old guy?" Heather asked.

"One of the coolest jazz musicians in the city. He owns a club just off Fifth."

"Jazz?" Heather wrinkled her nose. "How did you meet someone like that?"

"In the music store about two blocks from his club. I jam with him and his band sometimes."

Heather frowned at this but said nothing. Which was good, because Sid tended to be protective of Rake. She'd even gotten into an argument once in the music store when a punk insulted Rake as he was tinkering on a piano. Sam, the owner, had stepped in before it went farther than shoving and kicked the guy out.

The hum of voices and the odd bubble of laughter bounced off them as they ate, reminding Sid how little she had in common with her cousin. She glanced back toward Rake, sitting alone, seen by most of these Friday night shoppers as nothing but an old black man in an out-of-date suit jacket. They'd never seen his face glowing because it couldn't contain the joy of losing himself in music. Blissing out, Ten Pin had called it once. Sitting across from Rake, talking rhythms and riffs and the finer points of improv jazz – that was where Sid wanted to be right now.

The half-formed intention of telling Heather the shopping was over drove Sid to her feet. Before she could say anything movement in the corner of her eye pulled her attention sideways. Wes Remichuk strolled toward her, his arm around a petite brunette with huge brown eyes and boobs so big she looked in danger of toppling forward. Maybe Wes was helping her stay upright. Sid regretted the thought. Her first instinct was usually to feel sorry for girls with such big bust lines – most guys couldn't see past the boobs to the person behind them. How did they put up with the constant ogling and stream of lewd comments without resorting to carrying a baseball bat?

Sid hoped they would pass by, but she should have known better with the way her luck was running this week. Wes and the brunette stopped an arm's length away. Was he afraid she'd belt him again? He gave Heather a long perusal, his gaze so obviously pausing on her chest that her cheeks started turning pink. Sid couldn't recall ever seeing Heather get embarrassed before.

She cleared her throat. "If you're lost, the information booth is that way." She pointed over Wes's shoulder.

"Not lost. Checking out Joanne's competition, Romeo. Or is it Juliet? Do you say Juliet and Juliet?"

"I say, 'Get lost, dickhead.' This is my cousin." Sid's heart started thudding. She fisted her hands, wanting to give him a matching bruise on his jaw. He lifted his chin, as if daring her. She could hardly think over the urge to strike coarsing through her veins. Her fists clenched harder.

"Kissing cousins. How sweet."

Sid pressed her hands against her hips to keep them from rising. "Yeah. Make sure you tell that to her boyfriend. But only when I'm around so I can watch him grind you into sawdust."

Wes glanced at Heather again who wasn't even trying to hide her anger. His eyebrows rose in what looked to Sid to be false bravado. She knew she'd won this round without resorting to violence. Her fists relaxed. Wouldn't Brock be proud of her?

"Wessie," the brunette said, a worried note in her voice, "we're going to be late for the movie."

Sid smiled tightly. "Yeah, *Wessie.* You don't want to be late."

To get by Sid and the nearest table, Wes had to let his girlfriend go first. As he stepped past, he shifted and raised his elbow so it brushed Sid's breast. She inhaled sharply. Wes glanced over his shoulder and curled his lip.

Sid started forward. Heather grabbed her arm. "Let him go."

"Did you see...?"

"Yes. He's not worth getting in trouble over."

Sid exhaled slowly. She already knew that.

"So..." Heather said and tilted her head. "Is he the reason you've got the sudden urge to discover your feminine side?"

Sid hesitated. "Actually, no."

"Whatever." Said like Heather didn't believe her. She gathered up their purchases that had been piled by their feet and handed Sid a lingerie bag. "I think I deserve an explanation."

Sid knew she was right. "Look, this really isn't about Wes thinking I'm gay. I need to make a good impression on some guys in a band. They're cool. I'm on the fringes at best. Their leader told me it might help if I look..." Sid waved her hand up and down. "...like you."

"So you think changing how you look will change how people look at you?"

Sid shrugged. She didn't know what she thought. She only knew she had to get into that band. "What do you think?"

Heather suddenly smiled. "Advertising is king. Image is everything. And that means we have more shopping to do."

Sid groaned. "You said no cargoes, but at least tell me I get to still wear jeans."

"Of course, just not baggy ones like I've seen you wear. Come on. We'll get some right now."

"You know, there's a half decent music store in the east wing..."

"No. We're doing this my way, Sid."
"Yeah, yeah. Your way or not at all. Stop tempting me."
"You're going to love the new you."
"I seriously doubt that."

9 | hi-hat on the edge

"So," Heather said, "who do we test the new you on? Other than Uncle James, of course."

Sid hadn't taken her eyes off the girl in the mirror. A girl with pixie hair and a face to match. A girl with curves and legs. *This skirt is shorter than I remember it being in the store.* The girl in the mirror – an odd-looking stranger – stared back at Sid with wide eyes. She was kind of cute. She sure didn't look like a woodworking, hard-drumming tomboy.

Heather had arrived early, and with the help of a friend who was a cosmetology queen, had spent the day transforming Sid. They had cut hair, applied makeup, primped and fussed and taken pictures at every stage. But they hadn't let Sid see the results until they had her dressed in one of her new outfits, complete with matching flats. No way was Sid going to learn to wear heels on top of everything else. She eyed the skirt, lacey camisole and fitted top with a very low neckline that revealed the camisole's trim. She bit her lip.

"Don't bite your lip," Heather said. "Don't lick, either.

You want to stay glossy."

"Yeah. Glossy." Sid thought she looked like a china doll, which made her glassy, not glossy. No wonder boys sometimes thought girls were so breakable. Would this really help get her into the band? Sid hoped so; after all, the girls who hung out with TFD's members dressed more or less like this.

"We should do her nails," Heather's friend Coral said.

"I can do that with her tomorrow. I didn't want to overwhelm her."

Sid cleared her throat. "I'm right here, you know. And I do have ears that work. I'm not a giant doll you're playing dress-up with, even if I do look like one."

"Don't be silly, Sidney," Heather said. "Let's show Uncle James."

"Sure. Give him heart palpitations to go with his ulcer."

"Ulcer? Why does Uncle James have an ulcer?"

"I'm not sure he has one. He won't go to the doctor. But since his promotion he works pretty much non-stop. Evenings, weekends. That mutual funds company is eating him from the inside out and all he does is pop antacid pills and keep working ..."

Heather nodded solemnly. "Dad's kind of the same way."

"Dentists don't work evenings and weekends."

"Sometimes, if a patient has an emergency. And he has a partner who totally stresses him out. Now, come on." Heather grabbed Sid by the arm and dragged her down the hallway. She knocked on James's office door before Sid could back away.

James called for them to come in. Heather opened the door and pushed Sid into the office. She stumbled forward two steps then stopped. James hadn't looked up from his laptop. He held up a finger. "One sec, girls." Ten seconds later he straightened and spun in his chair.

And stared.

For a long time.

Sid started to shift from foot to foot. Agonizing moments passed. "Say something, Dad."

James stood up and walked forward, slowly, as if in a trance. "God, you're beautiful, Sid. You look so much like your mother..." His voice choked off and he returned to just staring.

Like her mother? She heard the tension in James's voice – the hurt. Her voice dropped to an uncertain whisper. "I'm sorry."

James clasped her upper arms. "Don't be sorry, Sid. I'm not sorry. Last night you went to bed a young girl. And now you walk into my office a young woman. The change..." He looked her up and down again. "I knew you'd do this to me some day. Grow up on me, I mean."

He liked it. Sid worked a lump in her throat. Part of her wished he hadn't.

"I knew you'd approve, Uncle James," Heather said. Her smile was victorious, as if she really had enjoyed the challenge. "We should let your dad work and phone your buddy, Sidney."

Sid nodded absently. She left the office in a bit of a daze, still not sure what to think about her dad's response. She robotically phoned Taylor, and asked him to drop by. The girls sat in the living room. When Sid suggested that she could drum a bit, Heather almost gagged on her tongue in her hurry to prohibit drumming while Sid was dressed up. Sid thought "in costume" was a better description, but didn't argue. She'd do what she wanted once Heather left.

Coral and Heather chatted. Sid paid no attention. She couldn't get over her dad's reaction. He liked it. More than liked. And Heather thought she looked good. Sid tapped a jittery rhythm on her thighs. She wasn't sure what she thought. Mostly she was shocked. She had never imagined that someone who looked like that girl in the mirror could possibly live inside her.

Let the guys in the band be impressed.

The doorbell rang. Sid jumped up. Heather intercepted her and sent her back to the sofa, then invited Taylor in. He gave her a "what are you doing here?" kind of look. He'd met her a few times and shared Sid's conviction that Heather was a snobbish, fashion-obsessed airhead.

Taylor scanned the room, his gaze taking in Sid and Coral in a single sweep before returning to Heather. "So where's –"

He seemed to freeze, like a cartoon character that has run off a cliff and suddenly realizes he's about to fall. Sid started across the room. The movement drew Taylor's attention. He gaped. In her mind, Sid saw the cartoon character's jaw drop to the floor and his eyes pop out of their sockets before a bungee cord snapped them back into place. Sid wanted to laugh, except there was something so not funny about the whole thing that she felt like she might start crying. But she never cried.

She whispered, "Hi, Tay."

His silence muffled the whole room. With painfully slow steps he circled around Sid. His harsh breathing was like sandpaper in her ears. The smell of grease wafted from him and she knew he had been working on his motorcycle.

He came full circle and stopped an arm's length away. He rubbed his nose, leaving a dark smudge in the crease of his nostril. "This isn't a joke? You *let* her do this to you?"

Heather side-stepped so she stood shoulder-to-shoulder with Sid. "Of course she let me do this. She practically *begged* me to help her. Doesn't she look fantastic?"

Taylor exhaled and pushed his fingers through his hair, leaving a few black streaks in the brown. "I don't get it." But his eyes said he got it, he just didn't like it.

Sid couldn't find her voice. This reaction – acting like she'd been turned into a cockroach – was not part of the plan. Why was Taylor doing this to her?

Heather reached out as if to support Sid – left hand on left shoulder and right hand on right shoulder. "It's simple, Taylor. Sid is...the ugly duckling. You are a duck. She has, what's the word?"

Coral spoke up. "Moulted."

"Of course. Sid has moulted her ugly old feathers and stands before you, a swan. You are still a duck. You will always be a duck and so cannot possibly understand."

Taylor exploded. "You're so full of shit it's coming out your mouth! Are you even listening to yourself? You've turned her into a freaking clone." He spun, hit the wall, spun back to face Sid. "Is that what you want? To be another Heather? To walk like her and talk like her and dress like her? Is it?"

Sid swallowed, forcing a lump down her throat. The back of her eyes stung. "Don't, Tay. You know I needed...a different image. I'm still me."

"Are you really? You don't look like Sid. There's none of Sid's give-as-good-as-she-gets attitude. You don't even smell like Sid." His fingers raked his hair again. "Shit."

Sid couldn't remember the last time she'd seen Taylor this upset. He was Mr. Easy-Going. He was acting like a wounded dog, snapping and growling. Her legs shook as she took a step toward him.

Taylor pulled back. His hand waved erratically behind his back until it hit the doorknob. "I can't believe you'd do this. It's nuts. Phone me when you're you again." He gave Heather a scornful glance.

Then he was gone. The door's slam echoed through the room, and through Sid's chest.

10 | transition back to the groove

Sid sank to the floor, devastated that Taylor had blown her off. She had expected him to like her new look. He seemed to notice the girls at school who dressed like this. What was the difference? Why did he hate what she'd done? He knew why she was doing this. He knew how much getting into The Fourth Down meant to her.

Heather crouched beside her. "Ignore that idiot."

"He's my best friend," Sid whispered. Her chest still ached from the way he had fled.

"Some best friend. A best friend would be happy for you."

"I don't know, Heather. I...maybe I should forget it." Her best friend hated her new look. Sid watched her fingers drumming – no rhythm, just spastic little taps.

"No! He's dead wrong, Sid. And I'll prove it to you." Sid's curiosity surfaced and she looked up, waiting for Heather to explain. "Come with us tonight."

"Where?"

"Our guys are taking us to McGinty College to a concert

featuring some local bands. It's in their bar but they're opening it to everyone because some of the band members are under age. No alcohol served, if Uncle James asks."

Now that Heather mentioned it, Sid remembered seeing a poster at the music store. The concert was called "First Impressions" because for most of the bands it was their first time playing on an actual stage. Could be interesting, or very painful. She'd considered going when the posters first appeared and The Fourth Down was on the bill, but they'd withdrawn after their drummer died. That had snuffed her interest, especially since it was across town and she didn't like asking James to drive her places where he'd have to wait too long. It was too far by bus. Taylor and his motorcycle came to mind. Not that his having wheels helped her any, not after his reaction a few moments ago.

Heather squeezed her arm. "You have to give this a chance. It'll be fun."

"Totally." Coral said. Sid had forgotten Coral was there. She added, "My brother plays bass for one of the groups. That's why we're going. Heather said you drum. Are you in a band?"

I wish. Sid glanced down at her skirt and tried to tug it a little lower. Her legs were cold. "I used to jam with my brother's band, but he's gone to college so I've just been working at getting better. Taylor thought –"

Heather pulled Sid to her feet. "Forget Taylor. Tonight you are going to discover the difference it makes to walk into a room looking good."

Was I so completely awful before? Sid didn't say it aloud since she knew Heather would say yes. Maybe Taylor *was* being an idiot. Much as Sid hated to admit it, Heather was right: she needed to get out. She didn't want to sit around all night, moping about Taylor's outburst. Inhaling deeply, she nodded. Coral and Heather both clapped. Sid consoled herself that at least they hadn't jumped up and down and squealed.

The beautification project had taken most of the day, so The Guys (Sid couldn't recall their names) picked them up at Sid's and they went for pizza. The Guys did a great job at making Sid feel like the odd one out. She could have been a piece of furniture.

By the time they reached the college, Sid was in a black mood. The darkened bar, the flashing lights, and the crowd all made it worse. The only thing good was the beat. Sid craned her neck to see over the crowd. The guitarists looked like high school students, so she assumed the drummer was, too. She (or he) was decent.

Someone stumbled into their group and wandered off without a word. His wake stunk of beer. Apparently the bar not serving booze only meant people brought their own. Someone else bumped into Sid from behind, reinforcing her dislike of crowds, and the jostling most of all. Mr. Brock would probably say she was "protective of her personal space." Big time.

A guy with a goatee who looked like he had to be in college stopped by her and spoke. Sid glanced over her shoulder, assuming he had to be talking to someone behind her. Heather and her guy were swaying to the music – he was pressed up against her back with his arms around her waist. Her cousin grinned at her and yelled over the music, "Answer him."

Sid mouthed, "Me?" Heather nodded. Sid eyed the guy. "Were you talking to me?"

He nodded. "Want to dance?"

Dance? In public? Someone – it had to be Heather – gave Sid a little shove. The guy with the goatee must have thought that meant she had accepted his invitation because he smiled, took her hand and walked toward the edge of the crowded dance floor. He released her hand and started dancing. Sid stood for a few seconds watching him with a surprised detachment. He was sort of cute, for an older guy. And he had asked *her* to dance.

She hadn't danced in public since being forced to in gym class, but she knew how. She danced down in her drum pit sometimes. Alone. In the dark.

This is stupid, she thought. *Except for Heather, I don't even know anyone here. What do I care what they think about me?* Sid started to dance, tentatively at first, but then the beat took over. Except for breaks when one band left the stage and another set up, she was on the dance floor for the rest of the night, her partners a blur of faces. When the headlining group came on stage and the drummer kicked in with a hard-driving rhythm that vibrated over her skin, Sid threw herself into the music. She didn't care that she was in a crowd, didn't care or even know who her dance partner was.

She danced like she was alone in the dark, the throb of the drumbeat seducing her to let loose. She didn't even know how long she had been dancing when the music slowed to a sultry sway. She stopped in the middle of the dance floor and looked around, confused by the change in tempo, feeling like she'd been jolted out of a trance.

A guy with dark eyes and a five o'clock shadow stepped close, slid his arm around her waist and pulled her close. Sid stared, shocked by the intimacy of the touch. He smiled. "I like the way you dance. Are you good one-on-one, too?" He started to move his hips against hers in time to the music.

Sid twisted out of his reach. She trembled as she wended her way off the dance floor, looking for Heather and trying not to bump into any of the swaying couples. She found her cousin at a table by the bar, sitting on her guy's lap.

"Not dancing the last dance?" Heather asked.

"I'm ready to go," Sid replied. She picked up a half-full glass of cola. "This yours?" Heather nodded. Sid downed the drink. Heather's guy pushed his glass toward her so she downed it. A coughing fit grabbed her and she leaned on the table until it passed. "What was in that?"

Heather giggled. "Just a little rum."

"Funny." Sid glared at Heather's guy. "You aren't driving, are you?"

"No. Dean is. Don't worry, Miss Prude, he hasn't been drinking."

Another giggle burst out of Heather. "She wasn't a prude on the dance floor."

Sid rolled her eyes and sat to wait. The rum had burned going down; now a ripple of dizziness was coming up. Suddenly she felt like total crap: tired, sore, and thirsty enough to guzzle a fountain dry. She rested her forearms on the table and laid her head on them. What felt like seconds later, Heather was waking her up.

She dozed again on the drive home. In her room, she crashed on top of her covers without getting undressed.

The next morning she woke up feeling hung-over. Or at least she thought this might be what hung-over felt like. Swollen tongue, bleary eyes, aching feet. She wanted to go back to sleep but knew that Heather was coming over again.

Sid stripped to her underwear and snuggled in the thick blue terrycloth robe her dad had given her last Christmas. In the bathroom, she studied herself in her new lacey underwear, which wasn't very comfortable to sleep in, then took off the bra and panties and studied herself again.

Not skinny, not fat. A bit of curve in the hips. Small breasts that looked bigger in the kind of bra Heather had made her buy. Sid struck a sexy pose – and started laughing. Her hair stuck out five different directions and the shadows under her eyes made her look more like a zombie than a Playboy bunny. She pointed at the mirror. "*You* will not be wearing those stupid bunny ears any time in this life, girl. Deal with it."

If Mr. Are-You-Good-One-On-One could see her now, he'd realize she had only been disguised as a pretty girl last night. Not that she *ever* wanted him or any creepy guy to see her naked. Sid cranked on the shower as hot as she could stand it and let the heat cascade the soreness away.

After her shower she padded into the kitchen in her bathrobe. James looked up from his Sunday paper. "I've only had three cups today so don't hassle me." He squinted at the clock. "You do know it's almost noon, right? Usually you're dressed by now. Was it a good concert?"

Sid shrugged and sat down. "There was some decent drumming."

James smiled. "Nice to know my little girl hasn't completely changed."

"Yeah." Sid rubbed her eyes and wondered if today would be a good day to start drinking coffee. The shower hadn't done much to clear up the feeling of being hung-over. It was getting worse; a headache was starting. One shot of rum wouldn't do that. She decided it was stress. "Dad, can I ask you something stupid?"

"Sure. I specialize in stupid."

"Can a guy tell when a girl is wearing sexy underwear? Does she move a different way? Can he tell from the panty lines or the way a bra pushes up her..." Sid stopped. For some reasons, she couldn't bring herself to say "boobs" to her dad. Not this morning.

James frowned into his empty coffee cup. "Ah, maybe this would be a good question for your Aunt Kathy."

"She's not a guy. How would she know?"

James flushed. "I'm not sure how to answer you, Sid. This is very...awkward."

Sid sighed. Didn't she know it? "Maybe I'll ask Devin. Can I ask you something else?"

"Is it an easier question?"

"Probably not." Sid got up and poured some orange juice. She popped half a bagel into the toaster and leaned against the counter. "Yesterday, when Taylor came over, he didn't like my new look. Actually, he kind of freaked out."

"And you want to know why?"

Sid nodded and drank half her juice. Her bagel popped so she got out the strawberry cream cheese and spread it on extra thick.

"I can't answer that, either, Sid. It doesn't sound like the way Taylor would typically react. Maybe you should ask *him* instead of trying to guess what he's thinking."

"I don't think he'd talk to me. He was pretty ticked off when he left. Said I should phone him when I've decided to be me again."

"Give it a few days. Taylor isn't the type to stay angry for long."

The doorbell rang. "That'll be Heather."

"Do you want me to answer the door so you can go get dressed?"

"What would be the point? She's going to tell me what to wear anyway."

James chuckled. "What do you girls have planned today?"

"We are going dress shopping."

"Again?"

Sid started for the front door. "This time it's for the

wedding. Guys are so lucky. They throw on a suit, run a comb through their hair and they're done." She paused before entering the hallway. "Do you have any idea what a woman has to go through to get ready on a regular day, never mind what she does for a special occasion?"

James unfolded his lanky form and headed to the sink with his coffee cup. "I have a vague idea. I used to live with a woman, you know."

"Live with?" Oh, right. The woman who had resigned from motherhood. The one Sid apparently looked like when she was *in costume.* She wrinkled her nose and purposely kept her tone light. "With your age and how long ago that was, I'm surprised you remember anything."

James flicked some water at her but she was already moving. The doorbell rang again just as she opened it.

After several hours of shopping in new shoes, Sid's feet were screaming. She had never tried James's foot massage machine but she was eager to give it a shot.

While Sid's feet soaked, Heather outlined her plan of attack. The girl was thorough. Besides a laminated instruction sheet for putting on makeup and styling hair, she had written up a list of what Sid was to wear to school each day this week, listing underwear and bangles and colour of eye shadow. She had even talked her guy into swinging by a few minutes early so they could drive Sid to school every morning. *To keep tabs on me,* Sid thought.

By the time Heather left, Sid was definitely feeling nervous. It was one thing to play dress-up on the weekend, but to actually go to school like this? Was she crazy?

No, as Heather liked to point out, she was desperate. She was going to prove to the band that she wouldn't embarrass them if she was their drummer. The reinvention plan was moving forward. And with Heather's help, it had shifted into high gear.

Now Sid felt more than nervous; she felt sick. Before she retreated to the basement to drum the uneasiness away, she called Devin to ask him her underwear question.

He laughed. "You are in a weird head space lately, Sid."

"Answer the question. Do guys know when girls are wearing lace?"

"Not if nothing is showing. We just live in hope, little sis. We live in hope."

Now it was Sid's turn to laugh. When she headed to her drum kit, the nervousness was gone. Sure, Heather was helping, but this was still her plan. She had it all under control.

11 | single stroke roll

Sid had followed Heather's instructions to the letter, only jamming the mascara brush into her eye twice. It was weird to look into the mirror and see someone James said looked like her long-forgotten mother. She wondered if she should feel sad. Or lonely.

Mostly what she felt was exposed. The skirt felt too high and the top too low. When had she *ever* worn a top that showed cleavage? Even her bathing suit didn't. It wasn't much, barely any, but it was enough to make Sid feel like she had a flashing sign and arrow just below her neck that said, "Look here!"

Once she got to school guys *were* looking. So were girls. Even the teachers did double takes, if they recognized her at all. It was a good thing the blue top didn't clash with red, because Sid figured her face had to be scarlet.

The lunch bell rang. Sid tried to hurry through the crowded hallways. She seemed to be getting bumped more often than usual. A few times she thought she felt fingers brush her legs, but when she turned no one was looking her way. She made it to her locker and hurled her books onto the top shelf. She got her lunch bag out of her backpack – relieved that she had planned ahead so she wouldn't have to eat in the cafeteria – and jammed her combination lock back into place. Before she could spin the dial, a body thumped up against her locker.

She startled and took a step back. Wes Remichuk grinned at her. "New look. Heard about it but didn't believe it, so here I am."

"Here you are. In my way."

"What's your hurry? Hot lunch date? That why you're –" His gaze dropped to Sid's neckline and lingered. "Who knew? You have boobs." He shouted, "Hey, everyone! Sid Crowley has boobs!"

Up and down the hall, guys cheered. A few shrill wolf whistles cut through the din. Sid was certain that Wes had planned this but heat still scorched her cheeks. She started to walk away. Fingers tickled her thigh. She wheeled and plowed her fist toward Wes. His cupped hand caught hers and he squeezed, a grin telling Sid he had expected her reaction.

"That isn't very lady-like. Got to play the part if you're going to dress it, babe." He released her hand and walked away, whistling.

Sid watched him go, her stomach a boiling stew of fury, embarrassment and confusion. She hated the way Wes said *babe.* She beetled to the library to eat her lunch in private and to regain enough calm to face her afternoon classes. It might be easier if she could talk to Taylor, but they didn't share any classes and the one time she had seen him, before classes, he had turned away and started talking with someone. All she'd done was change the way she dressed. Was that criminal? How was she supposed to ask Taylor what was wrong when he wouldn't look at her?

While she was wasting time in the music section of the stacks, someone came up behind her. Sid turned. Stared. Closed the voluminous *Rock and Roll Year By Year* and hugged it against her chest. Mousy, Rocklin had said. Joanne wasn't, not really. Her hair was maybe mouse-coloured, but clean and soft looking. She didn't wear makeup but her face was clear, cheeks rosy. *Clean-cut,* Sid thought.

Joanne held up a hand and whispered, "Don't freak on me, Sid. I'm not here to get rejected a second time." Sid continued to stare. Joanne released a slow breath. "I just needed to tell you...that you don't need to do this." She waved her hand up and down. "You always looked so confident before. You'd walk down the hall saying hi to people, saying "He's rockin,'" when anyone asked about your brother. You're not afraid to look anyone in the eye. I only feel like that on the court. Today you look, I don't know, awkward." She'd grown increasingly anguished-looking as she spoke, as if it were costing her a lot to say anything at all.

Sid licked her dry bottom lip, then remembered Heather's admonition to not lick. "Takes time to get used to a new style."

"I hope I don't have anything to do with this. A friend

told me you might be interested, otherwise I'd never have... This new style isn't you freaking out over that party, is it?"

Sid shook her head. "I just need to fit in, for other reasons."

"You did fit in." Joanne turned and walked away with the lithe grace of an athlete.

Sid frowned. Maybe she did fit in, but not with the guys who counted. Not with the guys who could give her the break she needed to get on stage.

History class was a drag. Sid was relieved to get to the shop and finish up her project so she could take it home for the wedding this weekend. She ignored everyone, though it was difficult because she could feel the stares. She even caught Mr. Franklin looking at her oddly.

Halfway through the class she developed a case of dropsy. A screwdriver hit the floor first and she bent down to pick it up. She immediately realized her mistake and looked around to see half the class watching her. Wes gave her a wolfish grin as if silently telling her how much he liked blue lace.

Next to fall was a chisel she had been using to level off one foot of the bridal chest. She considered it with dismay, then knees clamped together, awkwardly inched down into a crouch, going only far enough for her fingers to pinch the chisel and get it off the floor. Then she bumped her pile of sandpaper and several pieces fell to the floor. Maybe she could go down on her knees, but then how would she get back up? Rick appeared at her side and scooped up the abrasive sheets. She mouthed, *Thank you.* He smiled.

He returned to his station and Wes took his place. "I like it better when you bend over."

"Leave me alone, Wes."

"What's this change for, anyway? Got some hot gay chick you're trying to impress? Or are you hoping to sleep with Rock to get the drummer spot?" He leaned close, so close they could have been getting ready to slow dance. "Way too little, way too late, babe. I was talking to him just after we met at lunch. He's going to give me a trial run. I'll be practising with the band all week."

"You're lying."

He grinned. "Don't have to. But don't worry, dressed like this you can always apply to be a groupie." His fingers touched her leg just below her skirt's hem.

Sid spun and charged out of class. It was either that or deck Wes again. She heard Mr. Franklin call for her to come back, but she veered into the nearest bathroom, locked herself in a cubicle and sat down. Her legs were shaking. *He's lying. He has to be lying.*

When the bell rang, she still hadn't moved, but at least she had stopped shaking. Girls came into the bathroom in small flocks, laughing and talking in animated voices. Sid listened, expecting to hear her name, expecting it to be accompanied by hysterical giggles, straining for word of TFD. It didn't happen. She stayed where she was until the bathroom was silent, left the cubicle to wash her hands and splash water on her face. She frowned at the smears of colour her makeup left on the paper towel, tossed it and crept into almost empty hallways.

No one was near her locker. She stuffed books in her backpack, relocked the door and looked up to see Mr. Brock walking toward her. He was strolling, like his route was accidental, but his face was a mixture of sympathy and concern. Sid headed toward the nearest exit, her strides long and probably totally inappropriate for someone wearing a skirt. She didn't care. To her surprise, Brock didn't order her to stop, to demand an accounting or a confession or a sob story.

She charged outside. A block away from the school, the low clouds began to spit and sputter. A perfect ending to the day. The spitting increased to a steady drizzle.

Sid hadn't thought to bring a coat this morning. She walked home, the rain plastering her clothes to her skin and washing away the rest of her mask.

12 | double bass triplets

Getting up on Tuesday morning and following Heather's directions for what to wear was painful. Sid might have abandoned her plan except for two things: she didn't have to wear a skirt today and she was sure Wes was bluffing. Because they all knew she was the better drummer.

She examined herself in the mirror. Tight jeans instead of her usual baggy ones, and a scoop-necked red T-shirt that hugged her body and would have showed off a lot of boob if not for the white lace of a camisole. Sid doubted her hair and makeup were done to Heather's standards, but since she had never bothered with any of that before the plan, the result was still surprisingly feminine. She wondered if this process would get less painful. Her right eye still stung from being jabbed with the mascara brush.

She slid her feet into the same navy flats she had worn yesterday. The shoes, at least, were getting comfortable. She sighed. Was this work worth the effort? Would the guys from TFD even notice that she was no longer an embarrassment?

Imposter, said a tiny voice in her head. *Shut up,* she replied and left to face the day.

At the sidewalk, she reflexively glanced toward Taylor's house and saw him walking down the driveway. She quickened her steps. The *slap, slap, slap* of her shoes against the cement annoyed her. She was used to sneakers and the way they let you, well, sneak.

Beside Sid, a horn honked. She started. Taylor looked her way and for a long moment they stared at each other. Then Taylor turned away and Heather called out the window of her guy's car, "Hey, Sid, get in. We're running late and I have a chem test."

Sid frowned at Taylor's retreating form, then climbed into the silver Honda's back seat.

Heather peeked around her headrest. "How was yesterday?"

"Don't ask."

Heather scowled prettily. "I just did."

Sid returned the look. "You never told me that short skirts make guys think you want your legs stroked." She kept her other thought to herself, that Heather hadn't warned her to not bend over in a skirt. She didn't want her cousin to know how clueless she was about what should have been obvious.

Heather smirked but said nothing. She faced front again and turned up the stereo. A rap song – Eminem, Sid thought – filled the silence. Sid crossed her arms and sank down in her seat. What she wouldn't give for some hard-driving metal or a little Rush to cheer her up.

As she was getting out of the car across from the school, Heather's guy said, "You look good." Like Heather hadn't told him to say that.

"It's all my doing," Heather said.

"I know, babe."

They kissed. Sid snorted and walked away, wondering about the difference between the affectionate way he said *babe* and the condescending way Wes had said it. It almost made Sid feel sorry for Wes's busty girlfriend. Was she anything more than a big set of boobs to him?

Not many people were in the wing with Sid's locker. She put away all her books except for math. Her most hated class. At least she got it out of the way early each day. As she was spinning the combination lock's dial, Mr. Brock stopped beside her. Hardly an accident.

"How are you doing, Sidney?"

"Fine."

He gave her a moment to expand but she didn't. He nodded. "Good. I still expect to see you on Thursday during last class." Right, the *touching base* session. He gave her a gentle smile that she supposed was intended to inspire confidence and headed toward the office. A few steps down the hall, he halted and glanced back. "By the way, you look nice today."

At that, the few people who were nearby all paused and stared at Sid. She felt her cheeks warming and retreated, shoes clacking on the linoleum. She wanted to run home and change into her favourite baggy, stone-washed jeans and In Flames T-shirt. But that would mean giving up on the plan. She should have known it would take people a while to get used to her new look. Change always made people take notice. Next week she'd be yesterday's news. Next week the band would have realized she could do *cool* and she'd be part of their fold.

She was in the math classroom before the hallways got crowded. During break, as she made her way to her locker to exchange math books for bio, a few guys brushed against her. She thought she heard a whisper: "Show us your colours."

That was stupid. There wasn't any gang activity in this school. The communities that fed into the high school were middle or upper-middle class. Over-achievers were common; gangs of any stripe not so much. And strict rules about wearing gang colours kept things that way. Every year, a group of parents tried to press the idea of school uniforms. To Sid's relief, they had yet to win the vote. The thought of jackets and plaid skirts were enough to make her want to puke.

After bio, Sid braved the cafeteria for lunch. It was already buzzing when she arrived. Another whisper, the same whisper, reached her ears. "Show us your colours." Scowling, Sid got in line for a helping of overcooked chicken fingers. She slopped some dipping sauce onto her plate and asked for a scoop of tossed salad which she covered in a thick layer of Ranch dressing.

As she waited for her turn at the till, a hand cupped her left butt cheek. She gasped and was about to dodge when breath stirred her hair with a whispered, "Show us your colours, babe."

Sid suddenly understood: colours referred to her panties. She turned and faced Wes Remichuk. She gave him a faint smile. "Touch me like that again and I'll kick your balls through the window."

He winced, then laughed. "I'd rather you do something else with them."

Sid tipped her tray and shoved it against his chest.

"Hey!" Wes jumped back and the person behind him spilled his tray against Wes's back.

Sid walked away as Wes began to swear. She spotted Taylor sitting by himself in the corner to the left of the main doors and veered toward him. He watched her with something like dismay wrinkling his forehead. But at least he didn't run away.

She sat across from him and soaked in his presence. She hadn't realized how much it added to her peace of mind, almost as much as being able to talk to Devin. His tan cheeks were underlaid with a distinct pink tone. Was he embarrassed?

Sid's stomach growled. Taylor said nothing. Narain sat beside him and Taylor looked relieved. Sid had always liked how they blended, stepping stones from Narain's dark to her light with Taylor in the middle. Sid frowned and glanced toward the cafeteria line-up where a server was helping Wes get cleaned up. A teacher's shadow fell across Sid.

Mr. Franklin, looking pasty under the fluorescent lighting, said, "You have to pay for your lunch, Sidney, however you choose to dispose of it."

He was being very calm. Sid figured he must have seen what happened. She handed him a ten-dollar bill. "Keep the change."

Franklin tugged his scraggly beard then took the money, shook his head and walked away. Sid sighed. No doubt he'd report to Mr. Brock. She was going to face a lot of questions in that next counselling session. Which was massively irritating considering it was Wes's mouth and Wes's hands that kept getting her into trouble.

Narain slid his tray into the middle of the table and motioned for Sid to help herself. "Are you trying to make an enemy of Wes and his pals?"

"He grabbed my a..." Sid glanced at Taylor, who looked suddenly pale. "My butt."

Taylor still hadn't said a word. Narain seemed to notice the awkward silence and tried to fill it with a jumble of words – about classes, the basketball camp he had signed up to attend in July, the movie he saw on the weekend. When he commented on Sid's new look and said he liked it, Taylor pushed back from the table and rushed, head down, toward the exit. He collided with a huge wall of flesh, bounced off it and kept trucking, not slowing to hear the football player he'd hit call him down or the laughter that followed.

Sid felt as puzzled as Narain looked. She asked, "What's up with Tay, Narain? He's been like this ever since he freaked out on me on Saturday."

Narain pushed his tray all the way across the table. "Eat. I'll track him down."

Sid nibbled at a chicken finger but her appetite was fading fast. She never much liked eating in the cafeteria. It was tolerable if you had someone to sit with, but when you were by yourself, trapped in a bubble of silence while noise ricocheted around you, reminding you that you weren't just sitting by yourself – you were *alone* and alone was the fate of social outcasts – then it became an endurance test, one that you wanted to finish as fast as possible. Better to stride down the halls, looking like you were on your way to meet someone, even if all you were doing was going to hide in the library, than to sit alone and have your status confirmed.

She dropped the dried-out tip of a chicken finger and rose. Two steps from the table, Wes cut her off, looking ready to wrap his fingers around her neck. Before he could say anything, Mr. Franklin joined them. "Here's your change, Sidney." He held out the money.

Sid glanced from the cash to Wes and back. She scooped the money from Franklin's hand and shoved it into her pocket. Or tried to. Not being used to wearing such tight jeans, she had to work at it for a second or two.

Franklin clapped his hand on Wes's shoulder. "You should be more careful, son. Those line-ups can be easy places for accidents to happen."

Wes glanced down at his stained T-shirt. It had to be white. And the tab label on the sleeve suggested it was expensive. Sid used the distraction to escape, disgusted with how cowardly she'd suddenly become.

She searched the halls but couldn't find Narain and Taylor.

they were in?

Wes watched her in carpentry class with unnerving intensity. That worried Sid. What worried her more was how often she saw Rocklin watching her in the halls, but not approaching. Did he like what he saw or not?

Evenings she would do homework and unwind on the drums. For a plan that was working, if it was working, it sure was making her feel crappy. Her drums were all that kept her from screaming like a chick in a bad horror movie.

Thursday afternoon, Mr. Franklin sent Sid to her counselling appointment a few minutes early. She was done the bridal chest. Franklin was disappointed she wasn't going to leave it for display but since her cousin's wedding was in two days, he gave her the nod to take it home.

On her way to the office, Jeff Clementine ambushed her. Pulled her into a recessed doorway and crowded up against her. His eyes were a flat, pale green, like a mountain lake on an overcast day. He didn't look like the bearer of good news.

"Let me go, Clem. I'm on my way to the office." She tried to free her wrist from his hard grasp, which was nothing like the relaxed way he held his guitar.

"I know where you're going." He leaned against the wall, trapping her in the corner.

Sid thought of Wes. Was he sucking up by ratting her out? "So let me go."

"I don't want a girl in my band."

"You said that last week. Rocklin calls the shots and you know I'm better than Wes."

He shrugged. "What if you are? That's not the point."

"What is the point? I'm late. Brock will come looking for me soon." She hated the way he was still gripping her wrist, his body almost touching hers, his breath hot on her cheek.

"The point is...I'm watching you, Crowley. The whole band is. A lot of guys have been watching you this week, which just proves I'm right. You'll be trouble if you drum for us." He shifted so his lips were beside her ear. "Who dropped you at school this morning?"

Sid got it. He was watching her very closely. But watching for what? She said, "My cousin." She hated the way his nearness was starting to intimidate her.

"Not your girlfriend? Too bad. I said it would be better for you if you were gay."

"Well I'm not. And I'm still a better drummer than Wes. Is it true he's getting a shot?"

Clem inclined his head.

"Will I?"

"Not if I have a say. And not if Wes works out." He released her, stroking her thigh as she stepped past him. She shot him a dirty look. He grinned. "Want to hit me? Or do you want more?"

What was his game? "The only thing I want from you is the chance to play drums."

Outside the counsellor's office, Sid kept her mind from her run-in with Clem by considering how she could corner Taylor at his house. She was pretty sure he worked at the garage tonight so wouldn't get home until nine o'clock. His mom didn't like visitors dropping by after that because he needed homework time. She had tried sending some instant messages, regular email, posting on his Facebook. He didn't respond to anything. Five minutes in his driveway was all she needed, just long enough to ask what was eating him. If Narain knew something, he wasn't talking. Ask Tay, was all he ever said.

Her fingers were tapping rapidly on the armrest when Mr. Brock opened the door and invited her in. Sid sprawled in her chair, then abruptly sat up and crossed her legs. Somehow sprawling didn't suit her new look. Her foot began to twitch.

Brock got comfortable and said nothing for a full two minutes. Sid could feel herself winding up, getting tighter. Twitchier.

Finally, Brock said, "You've been dressing differently this week. More..."

"Fashionable?"

Brock adjusted his glasses. "You don't look very comfortable."

"I'm sitting in a shrink's office."

"I'm a counsellor, not a shrink. So what brought on the change?"

Sid looked away.

"Okay. So let's say it's because of your run-in last week with Wes Remichuk. You're trying to...what? Fit in?"

"Is that a crime?"

"No, but you have to be true to yourself, Sidney. You look very nice but you also have to be comfortable. In your clothes, but more importantly, in your skin." When Sid said nothing he continued, "I hear you had another clash with Wes."

Sid was tired of the combined lecture and inquisition. She leaned forward a bit. "A clash? Is that what you call it? He grabbed my ass so I spilled my lunch tray on him." She sat back, expecting to be called on her language.

Brock didn't blink. "So Mr. Franklin tells me. Do you think you handled that in the best way?"

"Have you ever had someone squeeze your ass?"

One corner of his mouth raised. "Point taken. In case you're wondering, Mr. Franklin did address the issue with Wes. I believe he received two noon-hour detentions."

Sid almost swore. That would explain why she hadn't seen him in the cafeteria. Didn't Franklin realize he had made things worse? Her face must have revealed some of her thoughts because Brock said, "Maybe I need to have a session with you and Wes together."

"No." Sid jumped up. "Look. I have everything under control." Or she did, until Franklin interfered. "I don't want your help. I don't want anyone's help."

"Everyone needs help once in a while."

"Sure. And if I need it, I'll ask for it." Sid headed for the door.

Brock's chair squeaked. "We aren't done, Sidney."

"Yes, we are. This was just a 'touching base' session. Mission accomplished." Sid made sure to close the door quietly on the way out.

13 | syncopation

Sid had taken the coward's way out on Friday and had told her dad she had really bad cramps. Mention of her period always made him stutter. He'd been willing to phone the school and send Sid back to bed with a heat pad. As soon as he was gone, she had thrown on her cargoes and In Flames shirt and had spent the morning in the basement with her drums.

But there was no way to get out of Saturday. Sid was in middle of putting on her wedding costume and mask when she heard Devin arrive. The front door slammed. He shouted that he knew he was late and that he'd be dressed in a flash, but first he needed a shower.

More doors slammed. By the time Sid finished wriggling into the pantyhose that Heather had insisted she had to wear (to hide those hideously white legs), the shower was running and Devin was whistling behind the locked bathroom door. Sid banged on it and yelled, "Hey, Devin. We have to be out the door in half an hour."

"Yeah, yeah," came the muffled response.

With ten minutes to go, Sid was in the living room, more nervous than if she was walking down the aisle. She perched on the edge of her dad's recliner and smoothed the blue material of the dress. The tiny black polka dots felt like the material had goosebumps. A fringe of black crinoline showed along the hem of the dress and was echoed in the belt. The sweetheart neckline and spaghetti straps made Sid feel semi-naked. She had to force herself to not play with the necklace that dangled less than two centimetres above the neckline. Her toes tested the freedom of black sandals with unstoppable jiggling. They had a low heel, still more than Sid had wanted, and now she was wishing she'd done as Heather suggested and had walked around the house in them through the week.

James walked in from the kitchen, adjusting his tie. He stopped when he noticed Sid, his gaze flicking up and down. He smiled and nodded. They both heard Devin coming down the hall. Sid stood.

"I'm ready. I told you I'd be –" Devin halted by the front door and froze with his jacket half on. Ten seconds later he blinked. "Sid? Oh man, little sis, what did you do to yourself?"

Sid started to bite her bottom lip then remembered the stupid lip gloss. "It wasn't me. Heather gave me some fashion advice."

"Wow. I'm not sure I'm ready for my little sister to look so...so womanly." Devin finished putting on his navy suit jacket. "I'm not going to be able to enjoy myself now."

Sid frowned. "Why not?"

"'Cuz I'll have to keep an eye on you."

"Dad," Sid said. "Are you going to let him tease me like that?"

"All he did was say what I was thinking."

Sid huffed. She marched toward the door and almost wiped out when she stepped off the carpet. Devin caught her by the elbow. "Walk much?"

"Funny. Be thankful you're a guy and can wear comfy shoes."

Their cousin, Mandi, was getting married at a posh hotel. The ballroom opened to a walled garden where the ceremony took place. It was a perfect day – Aunt Kathy would stand for nothing less – with Mandi looking like a fairy tale princess attended by fluttery ladies-in-waiting, one in blue, one in pink, and the last, Heather, in pale green.

By the time the late afternoon ceremony was over, Sid's shoes were pinching her feet. Devin escorted her into the ballroom where the reception was set to take place in an hour. While they waited, the wedding party had pictures taken in the courtyard with its array of potted tropical greenery.

Sid found a corner, slipped off her shoes and massaged each of her feet in turn. Most of the people milling around were either from Uncle Peter's family or were their friends and neighbours. Neither Devin nor James were intimidated by the room full of strangers and visited with whoever was closest. As usual, Devin managed to be closest to a group of young women. Sid admired the ease with which he talked to them, and got them laughing.

She sat back and stretched her legs out straight. Someone in a grey suit tripped over her feet, stumbled toward her, veering at the last second, and fell onto the chair beside her.

"Sorry," he muttered.

"No, it was my fault," Sid replied as she tucked her unclad feet under her chair.

She glanced, expecting an old man, and found herself facing a guy about her own age. He had black curly hair and blue eyes. At least she thought they were blue – it was hard to tell with the way he was squinting. He might have looked like a model for a Greek statue except that his nose was a little long and his chin a little pointed. Actually, his face was a bit like a triangle topped by a black mop.

Sid realized she was staring and looked away as heat crawled across her cheeks. Then she realized he had been staring, too, so she looked back. What was a person supposed to say when she'd almost tripped a stranger? She held out her hand. "I'm Sid. Mandi's my cousin."

The guy dropped his gaze, lightly touched her hand then withdrew. "I'm, ah, Brad. Ah, Brad Dmitri. Mandi is, ah, was my neighbour."

"You used to live by Heather?"

"Still do. Mandi moved out about four years ago."

"Oh, right."

Brad continued to squint. Sid was starting to think she had a blob of mascara on her cheek or something. She excused herself, took two steps, came back for her shoes and carried them to the ladies' room. It was actually two rooms. The outer room had a sofa, a wing-backed chair and a wall of mirrors with chairs and vanities in front of them. And a chandelier. In the bathroom. Sid mouthed *wow,* and headed for the nearest vanity. An examination showed nothing obviously wrong so Sid moved to the sofa and stretched her legs out. Only when women started trickling in did she put her shoes back on.

A middle-aged woman entered and paused in the middle of the room. "Are you with the wedding in the Oak Leaf ballroom?" Sid nodded and the woman said, "People are starting to sit down for the dinner. You might want to get out there and find out where you're seated."

Reluctantly, Sid went, then was glad she had because it took her five minutes to find the right table. A minute after she sat down, Devin and a young woman joined them.

Sid whispered, "Where's Dad?"

"He traded with me so Lydia could sit with us."

Sid and Lydia exchanged unenthusiastic smiles. If Lydia worried about having to share Devin's attention, she didn't need to. He ignored Sid. *Why,* she wondered, *was I so excited about him coming home?* The other people at the table were older, friends of her aunt and uncle's. One of them knew James so Sid had to answer a few questions. Mostly, she picked at her food.

She spotted where the guy, Brad, was sitting, but even though he was looking toward her he didn't so much as nod.

What did she expect from a neighbour of Heather's? She studied the room as speeches started, then wore on. And on.

The oak walls of the banquet room were a perfect background for the white linen table cloths and chandeliers which looked like they were about to release droplets of glass on the heads below. A trim of carved leaves marched around the edge of the ceiling – the oak leaves of the room's name, Sid assumed. The same trim accented the bar at the back of the room.

"A toast to the bride," someone said.

Sid hadn't been listening but was sure this was the fourth such toast. It was the best part of the meal. She hoisted her glass of wine and took a sip. Maybe a bit more than a sip because her glass was almost empty. She topped it up, in case there were more toasts. A few of the older people at her table gave her amused glances. Devin cleared his throat and scowled at her. Finally, he paid attention, but only to disapprove. Sid stuck out her tongue at him and took another sip.

The master of ceremonies announced that the dance would start in thirty minutes. Sid raised her glass. "I'll toast to that." The man at the microphone paused. Had she said it loud enough for him to hear? He raised his glass and smiled at Sid. "Right. Time to party, folks." Laughter filled the room.

Devin took Sid's glass away. "I think you've had enough."

"Enough? Didn't you hear the man? It's time to party, big brother." Sid smiled broadly. She felt warm and relaxed and Devin was not going to ruin that.

"Go get some fresh air, Sid." He pointed to the courtyard.

"Fine." Sid stood. The first step was a bit of a wobble, but only because of her stupid heels. She raised her chin and wove through the tables to the open French doors. *Walk slow,* she told herself. Just like learning a new drumming groove; you've got to go slow before you can pick up the pace.

Even the night was made to order. Warm enough to go sleeveless, a few stars visible above the haze of lights. Sid twirled as she looked up at them. Her ankle wibbled. She staggered sideways. A man about James's age caught her and steered her toward a stone bench. "Better sit, missy, and let your head clear a bit."

Sid snorted. She was fine. It was the stupid sandals that were the problem.

Inside, a band tuned up. Of course Aunt Kathy would have a live band. Apparently they'd been set up behind some curtains that Sid had thought were just a backdrop for the head table.

Heather flopped onto the bench beside Sid. "God, I'm so glad that's over. Weren't those speeches brutal?"

"Guess so. I wasn't paying attention."

Heather laughed. "I noticed you gawking around. But at least you looked good doing it."

"Thanks to you." Sid tilted her head. "Where's your guy?"

"Mom didn't know who to seat him with, so he begged out of the meal. He'll be here any minute. He made big mileage with Mom by saving her that hassle, though I don't know why she didn't seat him with you." A smile lit her face. "There he is. Finally I can have some fun."

Finally she gave up and retreated to the library. No one there except a few students with their faces hidden by books, who looked up when she walked in, noses twitching like mice who smelled a cat. Despite her appearance, she wasn't a cat – and this was still the best place to hide when they were on the prowl, the one place they stayed away from.

When the bell rang to end lunch break, several of the library's inhabitants actually flinched. Sid knew that's how she'd end up if she didn't get her plan back on track. And a key part of the revised plan was going to be avoiding Wes. He kept making her look bad – and that couldn't be good for her attempts to impress the band.

For the next few days, Sid found ways to survive. Keep an eye on the crowd, zig into the open lanes in the halls, zag around any jock set members she spotted. Even if Taylor was sitting down when she walked into the cafeteria, he was always gone by the time she got through the line-up, so she sat with Narain and his girl, Lelah, and tried to look interested in her chatter. Lelah had apparently taken Sid's change at face value and now assumed she was interested in girl stuff. From Lelah's comments, Sid confirmed that Heather knew what she was doing.

A few times Sid tried to strike up a conversation with a girl in one of her classes, but it fizzed out in clumsy attempts at discussing things she knew nothing about. Sid couldn't even answer simple questions like, where did she get her belt? How stupid would it sound to say her cousin picked it out and she hadn't been paying any attention to what store

Heather walked swiftly across the courtyard, her stiletto heels clacking on the stone. How did she walk on such high heels without breaking her ankle?

Sid stayed where she was until the music started and everyone was herded inside to watch the bride and groom dance their first dance. They swept around the floor like they'd taken lessons. Which they probably had. Aunt Kathy didn't leave things to chance.

The bridal party joined in, then the parents of the bride and groom. On the second song, all sorts of people drifted onto the dance floor. Sid hovered by the French doors and listened. The drummer kept it tame. He looked bored. *Bet he wants to rip loose with a solo.*

Someone bumped into Sid. Grey suit, black curls. He turned. "Sorry."

"S'okay. At least it was actually your fault this time."

He squinted, then smiled. "Oh, right. Cousin to the bride. Ah..."

"Sid. Actually it's Sidney but only teachers and Heather call me that. And you're Brad."

"Yeah. Not good with names. Sorry."

"Are you going to apologize every other time you open your mouth? It's fine." Sid glanced at the dance floor where a slow song was ending. She wished Brad would move on. She couldn't think of anything to say. But he didn't. He shuffled his feet a little, like he was testing to see how slippery the floor was. The next song started. *Uptown Girl.* An oldie, but the song suited Mandi perfectly. Sid's heel clicked against the floor in time to the cheerful beat.

Brad shuffled his feet some more. His squint deepened. "Would you, ah... I'm not very good but... If you'd like..."

Sid narrowed her eyes. "The word is dance, Brad. Would you like to *dance?*"

"Would you?"

"Sure."

They walked out on the floor. Brad was a little spastic. She could see him counting the beat under his breath. She tried to get into the music but her ankles kept threatening collapse. Twice she bumped into people. Then Brad bumped into someone. What was he doing, making fun of her?

As soon as the dance ended, Sid made a beeline toward the French doors. Brad caught up to her. "I...was hoping we could dance more than one."

Sid planted her hands on her hips. "Were you mocking me?"

"Mock? Ah no. I'm just...not a good dancer. But it was fun. Wasn't it?" His blue eyes were in shadow and he looked vaguely forlorn. A lost puppy look if she'd ever seen one.

Sid released an impatient breath. "Fine. We can dance another. But I can't move in these stupid shoes so you'd better not have a problem with me ditching them."

"No." He blushed a deep red and pulled glasses from his inside pocket. "If you don't mind me wearing these at least I won't bump into anyone."

"You wear glasses?"

"Every day."

“Why not tonight?”

He shrugged. “My little sister told me I look better without them on, but then assured me that black frames are...nerdy chic, I think she said. I’m pretty sure she was mocking me.”

“Well, little sisters are pains. I should know. I am one.”

Brad smiled and put on his glasses. Square, heavy and black. Sid giggled. He said, “What?”

“I’ve seen kids wearing black rims, so your sister’s probably right. But on you...well, don’t hate me, but those glasses just seem...”

“Nerdy.”

Sid nodded. “You kind of look like a math geek, actually.”

“I am one.”

Sid grinned. “Where’s your pocket protector?”

“In my other shirt.”

Her jaw almost dropped. “You’re kidding.”

Brad smiled. “Yeah. Still want to dance?”

Sid nodded. They headed onto the floor. And stayed there until the band took a break. They conquered one awkward moment when the music slowed to a waltz by looking around and copying the positioning of a couple James’s age. *It felt nice,* Sid thought, *weird but nice.*

During the break, the caterers set out food at the back of the hall, but Sid and Brad decided to sit in the courtyard. She was surprised that they found so much to talk about. They both liked action and adventure movies but not the cop/buddy variety. They both despised peanut butter sandwiches, loved thunderstorms, wanted to try bobsledding, and disliked it when someone wore too much aftershave or perfume.

Their conversation continued to bounce all over the place until the band resumed playing. They were the third couple on the dance floor and stayed there the rest of the night. With each slow song, their embrace became more comfortable. Twice a guy asked to cut in but Sid refused. When the band announced last dance and started into a half decent rendition of *Unchained Melody,* Sid wrapped her arms around Brad's neck and his arms encircled her waist. Sid laid her head against his chest, closed her eyes, listened to the *thump-thump* of his heart, and finally understood the appeal of this kind of dancing. Their combined heat tingled over Sid's skin.

When the song ended they stood unmoving for a few seconds. Then Brad stepped back, his ears pink. He took Sid's hand, led her off the dance floor and into the hotel lobby where people were mingling as the dance broke up. They stood off to the side behind a circle of leather chairs and eyed each other in silence.

The pink spread from Brad's ears to his cheeks. "Will you be at the gift opening tomorrow?"

"I was hoping to skip out."

"Oh." His long face looked suddenly longer.

Sid felt a little lurch in her stomach. "But if you're going to be there..."

He nodded. "My folks are helping with lunch and stuff."

They stared for another moment. Brad's glasses seemed to magnify his blue eyes, making it even harder to look away.

Sid wanted to... She didn't mean to lunge. Her lips smacked against his; she knocked his glasses askew. She settled back on her heels, uncertain what to do or say.

He looked surprised. "G-girls don't usually...w-want to kiss a guy with..."

"I do." And she did. He might wear more-nerdy-than-chic glasses, but he was nice and funny and had even improved in his dancing to the point where he had looked like he was enjoying it.

Brad hesitated for another moment then lowered his head so slowly that Sid finally arched up. Their lips and nose bumped. They both flinched then, eyes open, began to move their lips. They drew back, tried again. Brad's lips were warm against Sid's, warm and wonderful.

Sid's hands found their way to his chest. Her eyes closed and her hands drifted up and locked behind his neck. When his tongue ran along her bottom lip, Sid almost gasped and her mouth opened. Their tongues connected. Sid didn't even try to sort the sensations rippling through her. All she knew was that her insides were melting.

Someone tapped Sid on her shoulder. She started and pulled out of Brad's embrace, wondering absently if she looked as flustered as he did.

Devin said, "Here are your shoes, Cinderella. Dad's gone to get the car. Be lucky he didn't see you or he'd morph into the evil step-mother." Devin held out one black sandal to Brad. "Were you wanting this so you can do the Prince Charming thing?"

This time Brad turned stop-sign red. "N-no thanks. I, um, better go, too." He hurried away.

Sid grabbed her shoes from Devin. "Jerk."

"Just doing my big brother routine." Devin grinned.

"Yeah, well you don't have to enjoy it so much."

"Sure do. 'Cuz you were enjoying it way too much, little sis." He pointed toward a multi-paned window framed by green velvet curtains. "There's Dad now."

Sid wrinkled her nose at him and marched toward the hotel entrance, glancing around in hopes of catching sight of Brad again, but she didn't see him anywhere. She never thought that she'd look forward to something like a gift opening, but now it couldn't come soon enough.

14 | flam with a dominant right hand

"Oh. My. God." Heather crowded Sid into the corner of the living room as soon as she walked in. Heather whispered, "I can't believe you danced all night with that total geek."

"Who, Brad?"

"Who, Brad?" Heather mimicked in a squeaky voice. "Of course, Brad. What were you thinking?"

"He's nice." And he kisses great, Sid added silently. She tried not to smile.

Heather sighed. "Why am I bothering to help you with this? Why would you settle for Brad when you could catch the eye of someone popular?"

Sid poked Heather on the collarbone. "I had to deal with a few of those *popular* guys last week. I'll take nice any day. Besides, he's kind of cute." Heather wrinkled her nose and Sid shook her head. "Look past the glasses, cousin."

"Let me guess. You're saying he's like Clark Kent hiding his secret identity behind ugly glasses? Give me a break. I've known that geek since we moved into this house."

"No. You've lived beside him. You've never taken the time to get to know him. He was never *popular* enough for you to bother."

"Like you know him so well after just one night of dancing. And necking. Eww." Heather's nose wrinkled again.

How did Heather know about that? Sid thought. Oh right, they'd been in the lobby along with everyone else. How could she get so wrapped up in a kiss that she forgot where she was?

Heather plucked Sid's sleeve. "And another thing, what's with this ugly T-shirt?"

"Starman is not ugly." Sid peered downwards. She had thought it a great idea to pair her white Rush T-shirt with the short skirt that had gotten her into trouble in carpentry class. She had rolled up the sleeves so they were more like cap-style and had cinched in the waist with an old navy belt she had borrowed from Devin. The navy matched her skirt and flats and the buckle matched the silver wrist bangle necklace. All in all, Sid was pleased with the effect. She smiled. "I feel way more comfortable when my neckline isn't threatening to cause a wardrobe malfunction."

"Impossible."

"What's impossible?" Both girls jumped. Brad smiled at them and repeated the question.

Heather snapped, "Where did *you* come from?"

Brad half closed one eye. "From next door."

Sid laughed. Heather spun and marched away, arms swinging. Sid said, "Thank you for rescuing me."

"Did I?"

"Oh, yeah."

Brad smiled. He had a beautiful smile that made his eyes seem to shine. Or maybe it was the reflection of his glasses. Sid tilted her head and studied him. He asked what she was looking at. She replied, "Have you ever thought about getting different glasses?"

A frown replaced the smile. "You sound like my little sister."

"Don't get angry. It's just that you have nice blue eyes and the thick frames kind of hide them."

"You think I have nice eyes?"

Very nice eyes, made nicer by a blue shirt that matched their colour. Instead of saying that, Sid started to make a snide comment about male vanity. Devin appeared beside them and introduced himself. He offered his hand and squeezed when Brad took it, making him wince.

"Don't be a jerk, big brother," Sid said.

Devin attempted to look innocent. "Just introducing myself. We didn't get the chance last night. Are you two joining the throng on the deck? The gift opening is going to start soon."

"How long will this take?" Sid asked.

"Judging by the pile of gifts, probably a couple of hours."

Sid groaned. "We just sit there and watch them open stuff for *hours?*"

"Don't forget the oohing and aahing. We are required to gush."

No doubt Aunt Kathy would punish anyone who didn't,

even though Sid knew she'd be gushing enough for everyone. Brad and Sid exchanged pained looks. Sid inhaled sharply as an idea hit. She grabbed Devin's left wrist and twisted it to see his watch. "Two o'clock. Perfect. We could go to Rake's and jam for an hour. No one would miss us here."

"What?" Brad said, his forehead furrowed under black curls.

Devin replied, "She wants to go to a jazz club and play music with some old dudes."

Understanding did not smooth Brad's brow. Sid smiled. "Devin could give us a ride."

"No," Devin replied. "I'm doing my family duty even if you prefer to bolt."

Sid shaded her mouth and spoke in a loud whisper. "Translation: the hot chick he was hitting on at the dance is here." She dropped her hand. "Come on, Dev. It'll only take a few minutes to drive us."

"I could drive," Brad said.

Devin and Sid stared at him. She said, "You have your licence?"

Brad nodded. "I'll have to okay it with Dad, but I'm sure he'd let me use the Jeep."

Sid beamed at Devin. "Problem solved. See you later, big brother."

"Dad's going to be pissed."

"Dad won't even miss us." She gave him a warning look. "And you won't tell him."

Minutes later Brad and Sid were pulling out of his driveway in a 10-year-old, slightly rusty Jeep. Sid gave directions to Rake's jazz club and fiddled with the radio until she ran across Metallica's "Enter Sandman." She cranked up the volume and sat back to enjoy the ride. Every time Brad glanced at her, she gave him a wide smile.

Rake's Piano Bar wasn't open on Sundays, but Rake's friends knew the door was unlocked so they could drop in. School work had kept Sid away for two months. She tried to keep from bouncing as Brad pulled into a parking spot across from the red door with green panels and frame. The old-fashioned sign of light bulbs that spelled out the club's name was dark.

She was out the door and around the Jeep before Brad turned off the engine. He climbed out. "I don't get it. Metallica on the radio and now you're going to play *jazz?*"

"It's all about the drumming."

"Oh. You said something about drums last night, didn't you?"

"Yeah." She took him by the hand. "I play them." He looked as if he were trying to decide if he should be impressed. He asked why she drummed. As she led him across the quiet street, she said, "It's all about loving the beat. When I was first learning I had to count it."

"Sounds like math."

Sid blinked. "I never thought of it that way. But after a while you don't have to count anymore. Then it's about feeling the beat."

Sid pulled Brad into the darkened entry. A coat-check room yawned to the left like an empty cave. Through the archway on the right, voices were raised and laughing. Sid picked out Rake's voice. "We here to play or to laugh at Jo-Jo's jokes? Ten Pin, count us down."

The clack of a drumstick against a wooden block silenced the voices. Drumming began like a bristling whisper. *Brush on snare,* thought Sid. She gave Brad's hand a tug and they walked into the club as the piano joined in, quietly playing in the lower keys. A saxophone eased in with a mournful wail that sounded like someone crying over a lost lover. The band was at the other end of the room, absorbed in the music. Sid didn't recognize the woman who sat on a bar stool in the middle of the stage, eyes closed, head bobbing to the music.

"Want to dance?" Brad whispered in her ear.

Sid smiled and turned to him, arms reaching up to wrap around his neck like it was where they belonged. Instead of embracing her, Brad rested his hands on her hips and created two hot spots that made Sid intensely aware of their closeness. She didn't realize the music had stopped.

"'Scuze me, folks," Rake called from the stage. "Club's closed. We be open again on Tuesday."

Sid slid her hand down Brad's arm and took his hand, then wove through the three rows of round tables to the dance floor where the lighting was turned up.

Ten Pin whistled at the same instant that Rake said, "Sid, honey. Is that you?"

"I told you I'd drop by soon."

"Never seen you in a skirt."

From his drummer's stool, Ten Pin said, "You clean up real nice, Sid."

She grinned up at Brad. "See why I like this place? It's like having a hoard of extra grandpas."

"Hey, now," Rake said. "Be nice. We aren't so old we can't admire a pretty girl. Introduce us to your beau."

Sid hesitated at that. She noticed Brad's flush. "Brad isn't my boyfriend, Rake. We met last night at my cousin's wedding."

"Uh-huh," Rake said, teeth gleaming in his dark face. "Nice to meet you, Brad. I'm Rake. That's Ten Pin on drums, Jo-Jo on sax and this here is Jo-Jo's new gal, Sonja. You play? We got a few more instruments over there."

"No," Brad said. "I'm just here to listen if that's all right."

"Sure enough. Or you can dance." Rake grinned again.

Ten Pin started drumming the same beat and the other band members picked up in the middle of the song. Sonja's voice started to weave through the music. No lyrics, just a string of words and sounds that seemed to fill out the sound, make it richer.

Brad shrugged, took Sid's hand and started to dance like someone their parents' age, the way they had during their first slow dance the night before. Sid understood. It was awkward knowing that four sets of eyes were watching. The song faded to an even slower rhythm, one that begged to be swayed to, and Sid had the feeling that Rake was playing matchmaker.

"What's with the singing?" Brad asked. "Lots of sounds

and, what are they called, scales?"

"This is improv. It's sort of like playing in a musical sandbox. No set music, just play as it moves you, see what kind of song comes out of it."

Brad tucked his arm in and cradled Sid's hand against his chest. "I could get used to this."

"It isn't always this slow. I think Rake is trying to make it romantic or something."

"It's kind of cool, having a band play just for you."

"Cool but awkward. Hard to get into the music with three grandpas watching you."

"We could shake them up with a kiss."

"I don't think it would shake Rake. I think he'd cheer." Sid eyed his smiling mouth. She was tempted. Very tempted. She started to lift her face.

The music stopped. Rake said, "You wanna play, Sid? Ten Pin's startin' to drag."

Sid smiled at his timing. Maybe a kiss *would* have shaken him up. "How can you tell if he's dragging when the music is so slow it's almost going backwards?"

"Don't you get sassy with me. Set your young man down and get up here. I wanna hear if you've improved any."

Sid snorted. Brad let her go and walked toward the nearest table. It was piled with bottled colas and water. Rake said, "Help yourself, son. Dancing can be mighty thirsty work."

In reply, Brad reached for a cola. Sid jogged up the two steps to the stage and snatched Rake's fedora from the piano bench. Ignoring Rake's mild protest, she plopped the hat on her head and took the brushes from Ten Pin's outstretched hand, then exchanged them for sticks and pointed them at Rake. "Let's crank it up."

Rake's teeth flashed. "Set the pulse, little drummer girl."

As Sid repositioned the stool a bit and sat down, straddling the snare drum, she realized that a short skirt wasn't the best clothing for drumming. Too late now. The bass drum hid her legs anyway. She tapped the wooden block to count down, choosing a moderate beat and tapping her toes on the floor to keep away from the kick drum which was often too overpowering for jazz. Rake started doodling on the piano, Jo-Jo and Sonja only two beats behind.

When they'd all grown comfortable with the low-key beat, Sid suddenly drummed a fill of sixteenth-note triplets and moved her foot to the kick pedal. The bass beat vibrated through her as she picked up the tempo. Rake didn't falter, matching the change. Jo-Jo followed Rake's lead and Sonja began singing an improv version of "When the Saints Come Marching In."

"Oh when. Oh when the saints. Honey, I said when the. Oh the saints come marching. Marching in. Oh-yeah." Off she went on a bebop string that had Rake grinning and bouncing on his piano bench like an old video he'd once shown Sid of the blind musician, Ray Charles.

Sid laughed. Her bare legs stuck to the edge of the throne's leather padding. She shook her head to clear some sweat from her eyes. The beat thrummed through her and the other instruments seemed to fade. She was alone with the drums.

She lost concentration for a second and flipped the beat, so she recovered with a fill of triplets and rippled the sticks over the ride cymbal, then dropped them to the floor tom. Drum roll, clash! Drum roll, clash! She sensed the band had stopped, but the new beat held her in its thrall. The drum solo she'd been working on flowed down her arms by itself. A few minutes of hard drumming and she let loose a double flam tap on the floor tom, then ended with a single hit on the crash cymbal.

She pushed Rake's fedora back on her forehead. Jo-Jo looked amused, Sonja a bit dazed, but Rake looked sad. Ten Pin sat down by Brad, pulling on a cola and shaking his head. Only Brad looked cautiously impressed. That was something, at least.

Rake said, "Honey, you know that rock noise doesn't belong in my club."

Sid stood and laid the sticks on the stool. "Sorry, Rake. I got carried away."

He sighed. "Head-aching, gut-twisting clamour."

Sid had never heard Rake sound so discouraged. Puzzled, she walked to the piano and laid the fedora on its smooth brown surface. "I said I was sorry. I was just feeling the beat. Isn't that what you always tell me to do?"

"Sure, honey, sure. You got to feel it, but you also got to control the flow so you don't start flailing like a chicken with its head chopped off." He pulled a handkerchief from the inside pocket of his plaid coat, wiped the hatband of the fedora, and set it on his white afro. "Jazz is fine, fine music. Playing jazz is like a woodcarver finishing a carving with tiny, precise cuts using his smallest knife. That –" He waved at the drums. "– was more like taking an axe to fell a tree. Ain't no finesse, just pound, pound, pound."

Sid huffed out her breath. "A lot of skill goes into a drum solo, Rake."

"Maybe so. But it sure gives me a headache." The skin around his eyes drooped like a Saint Bernard dog's; he looked so old. Something in Sid's stomach squeezed. She kissed him on the forehead. "Thanks, anyway, for letting me play."

As she stepped off the stage, Rake said, "You don't wait another two months to come back, you hear? You'll do better next time. I know it."

Sid smiled. Rake couldn't hold unhappiness any more than splayed fingers could hold water. Brad took her hand and they walked out. It had clouded over and had cooled off. Goosebumps shivered up Sid's bare legs and arms. "What time is it?"

"Three."

"Do you think we have time to go to my place so I can change?"

"Probably." As they climbed in the Jeep, a few drops of rain splattered against the windshield. Sid scowled. "I hope it doesn't start raining at the shower. Aunt Kathy will have fits."

"They'll move inside."

"While Aunt Kathy has fits."

Brad laughed and pulled out of the parking spot. He

stalled at the first corner and gave her a rueful grin. "Haven't been driving stick shift for long."

"You're way ahead of me. Dad's car is an automatic. When I get my licence I won't have a clue what to do with a standard."

"Maybe I could teach you."

"After you get a little better...?"

Brad's ears turned pink. "Right. So how do we get to your place?"

Sid gave directions and marvelled at how easy it was to talk to Brad. Almost like talking to Taylor, except she never wanted to kiss Taylor.

When they walked in her front door, she paused, wondering what to suggest Brad do while he waited. He stepped in close behind her. "Wow. Our living room is never that clean."

"Maybe because you actually live in it."

"You don't?"

"Dad lives in his office. I hang out downstairs." Sid brightened. "Do you want to see my kit?"

His brow wrinkled. "What kind of kit?"

"My drum kit." She took his hand and led him to the basement. They paused at the bottom of the stairs. "Welcome to the drum pit, as Dad calls it."

As Brad glanced around, Sid wondered what he saw. Odd pieces of mismatched furniture, a battered entertainment centre and bookcase that had been used as a cat's scratching post before they had brought it home, always intending to sand it down but never getting around to it. Even the drums showed their age. Sid had bought them second-hand and the only new piece in the kit was the floor tom, which her dad had splurged and bought for her last birthday.

Brad kicked his toe into the red shag carpet. "Nice rug."

"Maybe thirty years ago." She paused. "Oh. Sarcasm, right?"

Smirking and nodding, Brad walked toward the drums.

"Try them out," Sid said.

"I'd rather listen to you. You're pretty good." Brad veered toward the sofa and stretched out on it. He linked his fingers behind his head and smiled at her.

"If I don't go too fast. Sometimes I lose the beat when I try for speed. Rake's always telling me that I've got to slow down before I speed up."

"Why do you want speed?"

"Haven't you heard any speed metal bands? Their drummers are awesome."

"I don't think so. I don't know much metal past the big names like Metallica and Iron Maiden." He nodded toward her. "Rush isn't metal, is it?"

Sid glanced down at her T-shirt. "No. But their drummer is one of the best. Definitely the most versatile. He even has a DVD out on doing a drum solo. I keep dropping hints to Dad that he should get it for my birthday but he hasn't been hearing much of anything these days."

"Why?"

"He's stressed at work. Big promotion that has him working twice the hours. Brings work home. Usually he likes to unwind by cooking supper. Lately it's been, 'Fend for yourself. There's pizza in the fridge or meat pies in the freezer. I just need to finish this one report.' Which'd be fine once in a while, but now it's every night."

"Where's your mom?"

Sid had drifted to the sofa while she talked. Now she sat down by Brad's feet. "She took off when I was three."

"That's lousy."

Sid shrugged. "It was a long time ago." She wasn't about to let it start bugging her now, even if Brad was giving her a sweet sad look.

After a moment Brad said, "My folks yell a lot. So do my grandparents. I think it's the Greek in them or something. Lots of arm waving, too. Once Mom even chucked an empty coffee cup at Dad. Which made them yell even louder, each one blaming the other for what she'd done. I always feel like crawling under the furniture when they start. Maybe that's why I like math."

"Because it doesn't yell?" Sid spoke with a teasing lilt.

"Well, yes. It's quiet and logical and way easier to figure out than relationships."

"I'm not good at math or relationships."

"I don't know. You seem to get along with your brother."

"That's Devin. He could make friends with a rabid pit bull. I really only hang with my buddy, Tay, and his friend, Narain. And lately Tay's not talking to me."

"Why not?"

Sid frowned down at her bare legs. "He doesn't like my

new look."

"This is new? It's nice."

Sid smiled. "And it's even better when you take your glasses off and it goes all blurry."

"You really don't know you're pretty, do you?" Brad blushed, as if he hadn't meant to say it out loud.

"Am I?"

He nodded, ears bright red. "I can't figure why you're spending time with me."

Sid wriggled her way up the sofa, making Brad ease onto his side to make room for her. She took off his glasses and set them on her *Drum* magazine on the end table. "You really don't know you're cute, do you?"

He shook his head. "Ask any girl in my school. I am the math geek."

"Coo coo coo choo." Sid sang softly. Puzzlement curved his eyebrows and she said, "You need to sing that to the tune of 'I am the Walrus.' You know, the old Beatles song?" She sang, *"I am the math geek. Coo coo coo choo."*

His hand cupped the back of her neck and eased her head down. Their lips brushed. They paused. Without his glasses on, Brad's eyes were the deep blue of a warm summer's day. *Hypnotic,* Sid thought as their lips touched again. She was suddenly glad he wore geeky glasses because most girls would never see past them to discover the intensity they hid.

Butterfly kisses changed to lingering ones. Somewhere along the way, Sid stretched out beside him and ditched the belt because it was digging into her side. They shifted again and Sid found herself on top of Brad. The kissing went from mild and teasing to deep. They were both breathing hard. Sid's bones were liquefying. Heat pooled everywhere they were touching and she expected them to burst into flames. She *wanted* to burst into flames. Cool fingers slid under her shirt, caressed her back as they skimmed upwards. Sid moaned.

They stopped kissing for a moment, noses touching and gazes linked as Brad fumbled with her bra fastener. She wanted to reach back and help but his eyes held her immobile.

"Sid!"

Her dad's voice jolted her. She flung herself to the side and landed in a lump on the floor. James stood at the bottom of the stairs. His face was pale and he almost looked like he was vibrating. In a clipped tone, he said, "I think it's time for your...friend...to leave."

James spun and headed up the stairs, his footfalls thudding on each step, driving home the word, *leave.* Leave. Leave!

Brad sat up, ears so red they looked like they hurt. She crawled to the side, got his glasses and handed them to him. He muttered thanks and lurched off the sofa. He stumbled past the drums and paused, looking back as if he wanted to say something, but then he fled.

Sid just knew she'd never see him again. She pulled her knees to her chest and hung her head.

15 | backbeat

Sid couldn't believe she could go from feeling so hot to so cold in a few heartbeats. She hadn't heard Brad leave but she could hear James crashing around in the kitchen. How embarrassing, having your dad catch you necking with a guy.

Heaving a long sigh, Sid got to her feet, almost tripping over her belt in the process. She strapped it on and climbed the stairs on wooden legs that didn't want to bend. As she pushed the door open, a crash shattered what was left of her nerves. She glimpsed shards of sunlight spraying across the room. When she entered the kitchen she saw the metal ring and plastic handle and plastic lid – all that was left of the glass coffee pot – on the floor. Her dad stood like a mannequin with head down and hand outstretched.

Sid closed the door and leaned against it as she tried to get her heart to stop racing. She exhaled slowly. "That's a drastic way to cut back on your caffeine intake."

James flinched at the sound of her voice, snatched the bottle of antacid tablets from the little shelf that curved from the cupboard to the window frame. His hand shook as he opened it; pills sprayed across the counter. He plucked up two and popped them in his mouth, then stood with his back to the kitchen. His knuckles whitened as they wrapped over the edge of the counter.

Worry gripped Sid. She had done this to him. She got the broom and dustpan, swept up all the pieces of glass she could see and dumped them into the garbage can with a clatter. James didn't move through the whole process.

She leaned against the fridge and clutched the handle. "Dad, we were only kissing."

James salvaged another two tablets from the counter, chewed them and said, "You were about to do more than that. I saw where his hands were."

She sighed. "We weren't going to..."

"Don't, Sid. I don't want to hear your excuses." He turned and crossed his arms. Shadows painted a crescent under each eye. "Have you ever kissed a guy like that before?"

She scowled, not liking where the conversation had suddenly turned, but knowing she had started it so needed to see it through. "No."

"Then you have no idea how quickly things can get carried away. How easy it is to get caught up in the feeling and before you know it..."

She studied his socks as she felt his gaze boring into her. He couldn't think she'd –. They would've stopped. Wouldn't they? Needing to reassure herself, she whispered, "Have a little faith in me, Dad."

His socks came closer. His hand peeled hers from the handle and he guided her to the kitchen table. "We need to talk, Sid."

"You did the talk, Dad. Remember? The little book. You asked if I understood it all."

"Not that talk."

Sid was relieved. She got more than enough talks at school about safe sex and STDs and any number of things she really didn't want to discuss with her father. Not after just getting caught kissing... Her stomach tightened at the thought of those kisses. *Where,* thought Sid, *had Brad learned to kiss like that?* Did she want to know?

James gently pushed her down into her usual chair and sat across from, instead of beside, her. Sid waited with hands in her lap, fingers linked so tightly that they ached. For once she didn't feel like tapping any kind of rhythm.

James cleared his throat. "I guess I should have expected something like this, especially since Heather's 'fashion consultation'." It's a hard change to get used to, Sid. I'm shocked, but I'm not going to lecture you." Her shoulders loosened a fraction. He cleared his throat again. "What do you remember about your mom?"

Sid looked up sharply. "Nothing. I remember being mad and yelling for her, and Devin being really upset. I might remember the smell of vanilla. Was that her?"

James nodded.

"I don't want to talk about her, Dad. She didn't want to stick around. Period." She didn't want it to start hurting.

"You need to know why." He looked like he wanted to be anywhere but at this table about to talk about his failed marriage.

Sid felt the same way. "No, I don't. It doesn't change anything."

"Hear me out. I can't tell this more than once. I was nineteen and your mom was seventeen when we met at a mutual friend's party. We both fell hard. Six weeks later she was pregnant and I was offering to do right by her, whatever she decided. Her parents pressured her into going through with the pregnancy and we got married when she was five months along. She didn't finish high school."

Sid felt a heavy frown weighing down her eyebrows. "I get it. Don't play with fire."

"Let me finish. Your mom was a bit down after Devin was born. Post-partum depression the doctor called it. She snapped out of it and things went along okay. It was tough getting my business degree, already having a family, but we managed. Your mom worked part-time in the evenings when I could look after Devin and study. Then she got pregnant with you and was sick for over half of it. When you were born, she fell into a deeper depression than she had with Devin. Her mother had to come live with us for almost a year." James fell silent for a moment.

Sid had never met her mother's parents. They had disappeared as completely as she had. James had once mentioned something about their moving to Australia, but she hadn't asked about them and he hadn't offered any other information. Why should she care about people who cared so little for her?

James sighed. "She was never the same. No spark. Then one day, she just...walked out."

Unexpected pain swelled behind Sid's eyes. "So you're saying it's my fault she left."

"No!" James circled the table and crouched in front of her. "Don't ever think that, Sid. It wasn't you. She couldn't cope. She had been too young, or maybe she would have gotten depressed anyway. Whatever was wrong, it was inside her, somewhere deep where no one could help. She wouldn't let anyone help."

Sid's jaw throbbed. She forced it to unlock. "Why didn't she get an abortion?"

James stood and pulled her to her feet. "Don't ever say that, Sid. You and Devin are the most important people in my life. What would I do without you two?"

Sid sniffed. "I don't know. Eat fewer antacid tablets?"

He laughed, clamped his hands on her shoulders and for a second almost looked like he was going to hug her. "I'll be eating them by the bucket-load if you keep seeing that boy." Sid smiled since that seemed to be what James expected. For a second she wished he would hug her, like he used to when she was younger. She'd always felt protected from the world when his arms encircled her. He said, "Do me a favour?"

"What?"

"Have pity on your old man and take it slow. I'm not ready to think of my little girl..."

"Da-ad." Sid stepped free of his hold. Assuming they were done, she started toward the hallway and paused by the light switch. "Are the other grandparents still in Australia?"

"Yes. So is your mother. I keep in touch with your grandparents, sending pictures every Christmas and birthday, letting them know what you kids are doing."

"And *her?*"

"We still don't exist for her. Probably never will. It bothers her parents a lot. They'd like to know you better."

"Why didn't you ever tell us, about the pictures and stuff?"

"Because you never asked, Sidney. You closed that door as firmly as she did."

16 | matched grip

Monday passed with no call from Brad. That was a minus. But on the plus side, Heather was no longer escorting her to school and Taylor had actually sat at the same table at lunch without bolting for the door. He hadn't, however, done more than send unreadable looks her way every minute or so. Also on the plus side, she had asked Mr. Franklin if she could switch to drafting now that she was finished her bridal chest project. He had agreed so now a wall and glass windows separated her from Wes. On the minus side, the windows had no blinds and she could feel him staring at her in a creepy, gonna-get-even kind of way.

Narain had confirmed that TFD had let Wes do a gig with them on the weekend. Sid had been totally pissed off for about thirty seconds, when Narain joyfully added that Wes had blown it, getting so drunk he passed out between sets. He was sucking up to the band every time he came near any one of the guys.

So her plan was still going forward. If only she could

actually get near any of them. Not Clem. The one time she'd seen him in the morning he had given her a sneer that made her arm hairs prickle.

After school, Sid was halfway home when a vehicle pulled up beside her. Rocklin sat behind the wheel of a black convertible. He crooked his finger for Sid to join him. She did.

"What's your address?" he asked. She told him and he shifted the car into gear. He didn't say anything until he pulled into Sid's driveway. His voice was tight. "You heard about Wes?"

"Yeah. Too bad."

Rocklin shifted in his seat and gave her a mocking smile. "I'm sure you think so."

Sid shrugged. She couldn't deny that Wes falling on his face had made her day.

"So here's how it'll play out. You practise with us all week. 7 o'clock. My place. We just got a gig for Saturday. Some carnival day at a community centre on the east side. They had two bands booked and both cancelled. It'll be a brutal long gig. They want dance music for teens and a bit older. No heavy metal shit."

Sid didn't dare show the grin wanting to break loose. "I can do dance beats."

He pinned her with a narrowed gaze. "No drugs, no booze, or they kick us out."

"I'm not Wes. I told you I like to play clean."

He went on as if she hadn't spoken. "Clem told me you admitted you aren't gay. I don't care. Show off some boob, flirt with the audience, but don't even look at any of us."

"That'll be easy since none of you interest me."

Rocklin's sharp gaze was skeptical, as if he couldn't imagine any girl not wanting to fall down and kiss their feet. "You stir things up between us and I'll kick your ass off the stage." The corner of his mouth lifted. "Or let Clem do it. He's pissed off. Don't prove him right."

He shifted into reverse. Apparently the conversation was over. Sid got out and said, "Seven o'clock." She stepped back. The convertible whipped out of the driveway and tires squeeled as Rocklin roared down the street.

"The price of fame," Sid muttered. "Putting up with jerks."

Then she smiled. She knew they'd loosen up after that Saturday gig succeeded. And she'd told Rocklin the truth: none of them interested her in the least. The only semi-decent one was Han, but he was so quiet and such a yes-man that he was more shadow than guy. Why should she care about any of them when there was Brad?

If he ever called again after Sunday's fiasco.

As Sid turned toward the house, she noticed Taylor, standing beside his motorcycle and watching her. She raised a hand in greeting. He put on his helmet, started the bike and took off. He was headed to work, she knew. What she didn't know was why he was still not talking to her. Was he really waiting for her to revert to her old self? Narain wouldn't tell her what he knew and the way Taylor avoided her was driving her crazy. But she couldn't worry about that this week. She had band practise.

That sounded so good. Band practise. Sid jogged toward the door, eager to call Devin and tell him what had happened. He'd be happy for her, even if no one else was.

17 | tension and release

The week rocketed by. Each day after school, Sid had a light drumming session to warm up, made a salad for supper, went to the band's practise, then came home to focus on homework. No time to even think about Taylor's weirdness or Brad's silence.

Friday after TFD's practise, Han offered Sid a beer. She refused. "Come on," he urged quietly. "You've worked hard all week. You deserve a break."

She begged off. "My dad has a father-daughter bonding thing planned. Popcorn and a movie. The smell of beer wouldn't go over so well. Thanks, anyway."

As she left, she caught Clem's sneer but ignored it. He hadn't spoken to her all week. Had barely looked at her, actually, and that suited Sid just fine.

James wasn't home but the phone's message light was blinking. She listened to the first message, not surprised to hear James's voice saying he had to work extra late on a report his boss wanted for a morning meeting. Weren't these business types supposed to take Saturday mornings off and golf or something? She erased the recording.

The second message was from Brad. Not that he said so, but Sid recognized his voice instantly. So did her heart-beat as it sped up. He stammered something about having wanted to call sooner, that he had to go with his family to his grandparents' for the weekend, and that he hoped it was Sid who listened to this. The third message was Brad saying that the second message was from him, Brad Dmitri. Sid listened to the two messages from Brad nine times, then finally decided it was safest to erase them as well. She did so with a sigh.

On the off chance Taylor had forgiven her for whatever she had done, she called his house. When voice mail kicked in she hung up without leaving a message and told herself she wanted a quiet evening alone. A sappy romantic movie might be nice, one where she could imagine she and Brad were the main characters. Except...they didn't own any romantic movies and any she had ever tried to watch had bored her senseless.

She skipped through *Fellowship of the Ring,* only pausing at her favourite scenes, then fell asleep downstairs watching James's old VHS copy of *Gladiator.*

Saturday dragged as Sid waited for three o'clock to roll around. She got caught up on laundry, did the dishes and her homework so James couldn't gripe about anything. Not that he came out of his office to check on her. When a horn honked outside she had been dressed and waiting for forty minutes. She popped into the office and told James she was leaving.

His attention flicked down to Sid's red tank top with its scoop neck. She had agonized over whether to wear a camisole under it so it wasn't quite so revealing, but decided that Rocklin could be serious about wanting her to 'show off some boob.' It might only be for the gig but James's gaze made her regret the decision.

Finally he said, "Okay, Sid. Ah,...break a leg."

"That's what you say to actors, Dad."

He grimaced. "Well just have fun then. What time should I expect you?"

"The dance goes 'til eleven. Depending how long it takes us to pack up the instruments I should be home before one." Sid retreated before he could ask more questions. She pulled on her jean jacket, pocketed her house key and left.

Rocklin was waiting in his convertible, its top up in case the clouds got serious. He glanced at Sid's foot pedal box resting on jean-clad thighs and nodded. Was that for the foot pedal or the jeans? He only said, "Clem and Han took the van. We'll probably beat them there." With that he cranked up the music and took off.

No conversation suited Sid. She was nervous, but a good nervous. Ready to rock.

They had the stage set up by six o'clock. The organizers brought them a plate of burgers for supper along with fries and colas from one of the concession booths outside. Sid avoided the fries, not sure her stomach could handle the grease, and got water when she asked for it.

This was going to be a crazy gig. Play for forty minutes, break for twenty while a guy deejayed with canned music. Repeat three more times. Sid knew she'd be exhausted by the end of the evening. But the pay was good and the chance to prove herself was even better.

The hall had been cool so Sid didn't take off her jacket until she sat down on the throne. Han's eyes widened but he quickly looked away. Clem turned, stared at her neckline for a long time, then said, "Who's that for, Crowley?"

"Since you all play with your backs to me, you should know it isn't for you. I'll be sweating like crazy. I don't want to melt into a puddle."

Rocklin gave Clem a soft punch on the shoulder. "Play nice, kids. We're all here for the audience. They want a show."

Clem swore and took his position in front of Sid. Only then did Rocklin give her a knowing look. He remembered telling her to show some boob. He stepped up to the high-hat cymbals and repeated quietly, "For the audience."

Sid nodded. "I just want to play."

"Then let's do it. Give me a drum roll to get their attention."

The first set was low-key. Uncomplicated and easy to dance to. By the end of it the hall had started to fill up and there was always someone on the dance floor. One of the organizers brought them pop and water during their break and told them to keep up the good work.

Part way through the second set, while Clem performed

a riff on his guitar, Sid looked around and noticed a few familiar faces. Friends of the band. The jock set. She hoped Wes hadn't come. The organizers looked happy to have extra bodies, no matter where they came from. And they were dancing, which encouraged everyone else to get on the floor.

During their second break, Clem said, "Hey Crowley, is your ass sore yet? I could massage it for you."

Sid offered him a thin smile. "Only if you want to play the next set with broken fingers."

Rocklin laughed, a loud guffaw that turned Sid's smile into the real thing. Han winked at her. Before she could bask in the sense of growing acceptance, by Rocklin and Han at least, a few of the jock set joined them. Sid went for a walk because Clem was right: her butt was sore.

After the third set, they took a longer break in order to play the last forty-five minutes uninterrupted. The jock set joined them again, and Sid could tell that there was more in their plastic cups than just pop. She stuck to water and hung on the edges, only half listening to their boisterous banter. A few people complimented her playing and she nodded her thanks.

When they were getting ready for the final set, Rocklin had them gather around the drums like some kind of football huddle. "Okay, team, we've given them a good show so far. I want to take it up a notch. Can you handle it, Crowley?"

"Absolutely."

Her butt went from sore to numb after two songs. The crowd grew louder with the music, clapping and hollering their approval. Adrenalin kept Sid going as the energy rolled off the dance floor. They only had a few songs left when the chant started up: "So-lo, so-lo!"

Rocklin turned to face Sid, his fingers never missing a beat on the bass strings as he shouted, "They want to see what you can do, Crowley. Take the chorus."

Clem shot them both a dark look. So much for "we don't do drum solos." In response, Sid grinned and raised both arms high, sticks pointing toward the ceiling. The bass drum boomed. The crowd cheered and she flung herself into her drum solo with everything she had left. By the end – the double hit on ride and crash cymbals – she was drenched with sweat, but pretty sure no one had noticed the few slips. The crowd screamed their approval. Sid wanted to fall off the throne but managed to hold her sticks up in triumph. The crowd cheered louder.

They closed with two slow songs. Sid moved through them like an automaton, barely able to manage more than some soft brush work. When Rocklin said good night to the dancers, Sid staggered to her feet and sagged against the nearest wall.

Clem followed Rocklin off the stage. As they passed Sid, Clem said, "Don't you ever set us up for that long a gig again. My freaking fingers are almost bleeding."

"Agreed," Rocklin said. "But we did it so let's find some girls and celebrate."

Sid knew she needed to start breaking down the drum set but she couldn't move. Han walked over to her with a towel.

"Thought you might need this."

"Great. I never thought of it." The stink of her sweat reached her nostrils. Sid grimaced.

Han wrapped the towel around Sid's neck and patted at her face with a corner. "You did a good job. I'll vote for you to stay."

"Thanks."

Han still didn't release the towel. Sid looked up to find him staring down at the rivulets of sweat disappearing between her breasts. She tried to slide his hands off the towel. "I've got it from here, Han. Really."

He blinked and looked up. His cheeks pinked. "Do you... have a boyfriend?"

"Yes," Sid replied quickly, hoping it would soon be true. "He goes to a different school."

He didn't look like he quite believed her. "Well, if you get tired of him..."

"I'm flattered but you know what Rocklin thinks about that. Not if we're playing together." Since he still hadn't released the towel, Sid slipped out of its terry cloth collar and started dismantling the drums.

When they were all packed up, Rocklin took off with one of his cheerleader groupies. A second cheerleader claimed the other front bucket seat of the van. That left Sid on the bench seat in the middle, crunched between Han and the two tom drums wrapped in blankets.

Han had been drinking while they had loaded the van. He draped an arm across Sid's shoulders and held her close, to keep her from bumping the drums he claimed. When he started caressing her bare arm, Sid decided he was a bold drunk, but wasn't sure how to fend him off. She looked at him and whispered, "Don't." He responded by covering her mouth with his.

Sid easily pulled away, but noticed Clem watching in the rearview mirror. She removed Han's arm and nudged him hard, then spoke loud enough for Clem to hear. "I'm the drummer, Han, not your date. Don't forget it." She liked him better when he was a shadow.

He snatched her jacket from the floor, pushed it at her, then frowned out the window.

Clem smiled and cranked the music. At her house, Sid was stepping out of the van when Clem called her name. He gave her a solemn nod. "You did a good job tonight."

Confusion blanked her mind and Sid only managed a nod back. She watched the van roll away, still trying to figure out Clem's change of heart. Finally her mind kicked into gear. They all thought she had done a good job.

She punched the air and gave a victory yell. She was going to be TFD's newest drummer.

18 | slicing and dicing

Sunday was agony. Monday was slightly better, and it was filled with congratulations from a lot of the jock set so Sid's energy rebounded.

Clem caught her on the way into shop class and pulled her to an alcove outside a janitor's closet. Her good mood plummeted when he crowded her into the corner, blocking her escape with his body.

"What's up, Clem? You don't want to be late for class."

"I have study hall." He leaned close. "Relax, Crowley. I'm not here to hassle you."

Sid paused. "You're not?"

"No. I'm here to apologize for Han. He thought you were flirting with him. He doesn't push himself on girls. No harm done, right?"

Sid almost blurted her confusion. "Right. No harm. Can I go to class now?"

"In a minute. I just want to point out," he ran a finger along her jaw and continued, "how distracting a girl can be in a band. Especially one who turns out to be cuter than anyone thought."

"I get it. I'll make sure I keep my distance from Han." Sid forced firmness into her voice. "Now...let me keep my distance from you. Okay?"

"Sure. As soon as I've had a taste." Clem gripped her chin and kissed her while Sid clamped her mouth shut. What the hell was this? Another test? She glared at him, clinging to anger to keep revulsion at bay. He pulled away and sneered. "I don't think you're my flavour, Crowley."

"That breaks my heart. I so enjoy flirting with you." He stepped back to let Sid past. Fighting the urge to wipe her mouth, she laid her hand on his chest and fluttered her eyes in an exaggerated way. "A word of advice, Clem. Stick to playing guitar. It's what you're good at."

His expression darkened and she walked away before he could react. The late slip was worth it.

Tuesday morning Sid woke up feeling more cheerful than she expected, given that she still hadn't heard the official word from Rocklin about being in the band. She tugged on her skirt and a form-fitting shirt with a vee-neck that dropped a little lower than she might normally be comfortable with. After her mask was applied, with only one glob of mascara to dab off, she eyed herself in the mirror and adjusted the underwire bra. *I might look like my mom, but I have Dad's eyes. I can live with that.*

She passed Taylor's house as he was coming out the door. He spotted her and ducked back inside. "Coward!"

she called. The door cracked back open but Taylor didn't reappear.

At school the first person she saw was Wes, but he kept his distance, content to just glare. Hopefully he stayed away. No way did she want to land in the VP's office again. The last thing James's ulcer needed was another call from the school about her.

At lunch, Sid decided she had no room for food. She felt bloated and uncomfortable. If things ran their typical course, her period would start this evening. There'd be no begging off the regular math tutoring because James thought it had started ten days ago. Which was enough to darken any mood. How Brad could like math was beyond her.

She didn't feel like sitting with Taylor after he'd hidden from her this morning, so Sid headed to her usual haunt of the library, hoping the new *Rolling Stone* magazine was processed.

She turned the last corner before the library and almost bumped into Wes. He draped his arm across her shoulders before she could avoid him. She saw Clem looking their way. He disappeared out a side exit two doors down.

Wes said, "I hoped I'd catch up with you here, Sidney." He steered her toward the exit Clem had just used. "Rock said he wants to talk to you."

"Then Rock should've told me. What are you, his errand boy?" Still sucking up. Sid tried to twist away but Wes grabbed her arm with his free hand.

"Cool it, Sidney." He paused by the exit and turned her

toward him, his grip on her arm firm. "I've been a jerk to you since this whole drummer competition started between us."

"Aren't you the gracious loser?"

Furrows wrinkled his brow, then disappeared. "Are you so sure you've won? Playing good isn't the only important thing here."

Sid noncommittally lifted one shoulder. "Really? So is that what Rock wants to talk about? The band's rules of conduct? I think I already know them." Sid's heartbeat drummed with anticipation.

He gave the exit an uncertain glance. "Maybe you should just leave it, Sid. There are other bands. You aren't in TFD's league."

"And you are? You'd like that. Me leaving the field wide open for you."

"Maybe this isn't about me."

"Everything's about you, Wes. You've made that clear. Let me go talk to Rocklin."

He sighed, released her and gave a mocking sweep of his arm. Sid marched outside.

To the right, across the field, some students were using their noon hour to run the track. To the left, the members of TFD lounged around with poorly disguised beer bottles in hand. So the rumours were right: there was a drinking spot on the grounds, somewhere the teachers never supervised. There weren't even any windows in this stretch of brick wall.

Something about the situation struck Sid as not right and she hesitated.

Wes said, "What's wrong, Sid? This is what you wanted, right?" His conciliatory tone was gone and his smile wasn't the least reassuring. "Rock wants to talk to you."

She was breathing a little faster than normal, she realized. Her mouth was dry. This *was* what she'd wanted, a face-to-face with Rocklin. Saturday had gone great; she had nothing to worry about. She gave a jerky nod and walked toward Rocklin, who stood and waited for her. Clem and Han stood up but stayed behind Rock. Clem nodded in her general direction but it didn't seem to be at her.

Sid stopped two metres away and Rocklin crooked his finger, drawing her closer as if he were reeling in a fish. She was close enough she had to look up when he lowered his arm. He guzzled his beer and dropped the empty. The yeasty smell washed over her; she had the impression he'd had more than the one. She held her voice steady by sheer willpower. "Wes says you want to talk to me, Rock."

He nodded, moved closer, making Sid retreat a little. "That idiot wrecked our show once. But he'll never do it again. What about you, Crowley?"

Sid was tempted to look at Wes, but didn't. She edged away as Rock closed in again, almost swearing when her back bumped against the brick wall. "I didn't wreck the show. We kicked ass. We're a great team."

"Are we?"

Sid had no clue what he was talking about so couldn't think of anything to say.

Maybe it was the angle of the sun, but as Rock braced a

hand on the wall and leaned toward Sid his face seemed full of shadows. His breath reeked of the beer. "Stupid chick. Clem was right that it would've been okay if you'd been a dyke. He was right about everything. Why'd you have to go pull this shit?" His free hand flicked at her shirt's low neckline.

"What shit? You mean my tank top on Saturday? You were the one who told me to wear something low-cut. I've done everything you wanted me to. I made sure I fit your image." Sid's heartbeat was thundering in her ears but she raised her chin and met Rock's narrowed gaze.

"I told you not to cause trouble. But you didn't listen. Clem's right. Bands break up over chicks. This one isn't going to."

"What are you talking about? I'm not into those kinds of games. I just want to drum. I'm good. You know I'm better than Wes."

"Yeah. You are." He leaned closer. Sid had nowhere to go. Their noses were almost touching. "You have a boyfriend?"

Sid swallowed and nodded.

"Funny. No one has seen him, though we heard from a little bird that you were getting hot and heavy after some wedding dance. Why didn't he come to the gig Saturday night?"

"He was out of town. At his grandparents."

"That right? So while he's away, you mess with Han, then get huffy when he makes a move."

Is that why Clem had been smiling Saturday night, because he figured he had something on Sid now? "It wasn't like that. He was drunk and misunderstood..."

Rocklin cut her off. "And then you let Clem have a taste. Even told him that you like flirting with him. How stupid are you?" He slapped the brick. "Maybe I'm the stupid one. I believed you when you said you just wanted to drum. Did you lie to me? It makes me crazy, see? Are you wanting to play with us, or just play us?" He hit the wall again. "Before I kick you off stage you can damn well give me a taste, too."

Rock's mouth covered Sid's and his tongue probed for a way in. The back of her eyes stung. The tongue forced past the barrier of her teeth. Her hands wedged up to push the chest that was starting to press against her. His cheek crowded her nose and she could barely breathe. She tried to break free but he kept her crushed against the brick wall, sharp edges digging into her back. His tongue seemed to fill her mouth, almost making her choke.

Then she felt his paw on her thigh, pushing her skirt up, up. She struggled harder but couldn't break free. He squeezed her butt.

Tears streaked down her face, salted her lips. Without warning, Rock stepped back. Sid almost fell onto her knees. She leaned against the wall and gasped for fresh air. The stink of beer clung to her.

"Get out of my sight." Rock turned away. "Get me another beer, Han. Better yet, let's head to my place."

Feeling her way along the wall, Sid headed for the doors. She paused by Wes who was shaking his head. "I tried to warn you away."

"You knew this was coming? You helped set it up?" Sid's fist pressed against the wall. She whispered, "Asshole," and pushed away from the wall to leave.

The doors closed on someone's laughter. Not Wes's. He'd almost looked sorry for her. Almost, but not quite. Sid hurried to the bathroom and proceeded to dry-heave into the sink. Someone walked in. Sid splashed water on her face and looked up. Her math teacher, Ms. Pilson.

"I saw you running down the hall which is strictly.... You look quite ill, Sidney. Maybe I should take you to the office and find you a ride home."

Sid nodded and followed the teacher into the hall.

"What's wrong?" The teacher asked.

Sid muttered, "Something I ate, maybe."

One of the secretaries drove her home, clucking all the way. Sid thanked her and dashed into the house. She brushed her teeth and gargled. Showered. Brushed and gargled again.

She phoned Devin. "Am I a good person, big brother?"

"The best."

"I wouldn't play someone, would I?"

"Never. What's up?"

"I don't know. Everything's so messed up I could cry."

"Maybe you should. Listen sis, you don't want to tell me details, that's fine. But remember all that mush stuff: I trust you. I believe in you. Always."

"Thanks," she whispered. Then, dressed in sweats and a baggy shirt, she let the drums cry for her until, exhausted, she curled up on the floor behind the throne and fell asleep.

19 | closed hi-hat

On Wednesday, Sid wore one of her new pairs of jeans, but threw on her In Flames shirt. It seemed appropriate since she felt like she'd gone down in flames. She did a rush job on the makeup routine and didn't bother to do anything with her hair other than comb it.

Last night she'd avoided her tutoring session. A plus. Bigger plus: Brad had called. He'd talked to her dad first, apparently apologizing, then talked to her. Well, mostly he'd stuttered to her. Phone chatter wasn't one of his strong points, it seemed. But he'd called, and said he'd call again on Friday to see if she had any time on the weekend. In the minus column, her period was making her lower back ache. And she still felt completely crummy from her run-in with Rock.

She needed to tell someone about Wes the creep, arranger of great falls. Better yet, shout it from the rooftops. Except she didn't want to tell Brad. What Rock had done to her had tarnished the wonderfulness of Brad's kisses. It shouldn't have; one had nothing to do with the other, but thinking about it made her want to gargle. Again. The best thing would be talking to Taylor but she hadn't seen him all morning. She was so desperate that she almost considered going to see Mr. Brock.

At lunch she hid in the library. Joanne found her in the stacks. "I saw you this morning. You looked upset."

"Did I? I'll have to work on that." Sid pulled the library's only book on drumming off the shelf and opened it even though she knew it almost by rote. The conversation was over.

Joanne didn't get the hint. "Look, Sid. I know what this is like. Believe me or not, I'm offering my friendship here. Only friendship. You look like you *need* to vent."

Sid pressed her lips together. She heard genuine concern in Joanne's voice. But could she trust it? Unexpected words burst out. "Rock kicked me out of TFD even though I did a great job on Saturday, all because his jerk-off friends couldn't keep their mouths to themselves. He said it'd be better if I was a dyke. Want to date?"

Joanne stepped back. "You don't mean it. And you wouldn't want to live a lie just to play with them. Do you really still want to if the guys are hitting on you?"

"No. Yeah." Sid squeezed her eyes shut. Did she still want to play for TFD? How could she when they were all such creeps? The problem was that she wanted to play. Just play. And they were the only band around even remotely interested. A line from that really old limbo song popped into her head: *How low can you go?* "I'm so freaking confused it hurts."

Joanne's hand rested on her shoulder. "Do yourself a favour, Sid. Don't make decisions when you're confused." Then she was gone.

Coming out of the library, Sid noticed a handwritten sign on the wall above a fountain. Something about a video clip on the Internet. She noticed another on the way out of the school but didn't stop to read it. Probably an ad for prom. Last year's prom committee had done it and with the dance only three weeks away, this year's organizers were probably following suit.

On her way home, Sid decided that tonight was the night Taylor was going to speak to her. He didn't usually work at the garage on Wednesdays so he should be home. She did her math homework right away. Feeling hungry for something that didn't come ready-made out of a box, Sid decided to make some spaghetti and sauce, one of the few things she could cook reasonably well. She emptied a premixed salad into a bowl and added chunks of cheese and cucumber. In half an hour she was sitting down and eating. No use waiting for James; he'd have to nuke the sauce whenever he got home.

She rinsed her dishes and stacked them in the dishwasher. It was almost full so she added detergent and turned it on. She stood there for a minute, enjoying the vibration from the dishwasher against her soles, then headed out, grabbing her jean jacket as she went.

A fine mist darkened the sidewalks and streets, but barely more than that. Sid lifted her face to the refreshing spray as she walked. Taylor was getting off his motorcycle and pushing it to the garage when she got to his driveway. He didn't notice her until she was right beside him.

"Hey, Tay."

He stared, his perpetual tan gone, replaced by a white sheet.

Sid circled the bike and stood right in front of him. "This is stupid. Tell me why you're so pissed off at me." He stared. Sid cried, "Talk to me, Tay! This is driving me crazy! I need my buddy. I need to talk to you. I need you to give me advice and tell me when I'm being stupid."

"You're being stupid," he croaked.

"Funny. Please, Tay. I miss you."

"To talk to. To make you laugh."

"Well... Yeah." The words dragged out tentatively.

"But not to listen to."

"I listen to you. Make some sense here, please."

"You're selling out, Sid. It's been sickening watching you do pretty much anything to get into that freaking band."

"Not anything."

"Is that right? How much will you give to get what you want, Sid? I would rather you had let them believe you're gay to get the gig, which says a lot when..." His face scrunched up as he worked to continue. "...when some of us are, are struggling with whether we are. Or not."

Shock stamped Sid's features. She could feel it, but couldn't get her mouth to close, her eyebrows to relax. Words faltered, stuttered. "Some? You? But..."

He didn't answer. "Heather changed you into this, this

girl. When I saw you, looking so, so...freaking hot, it sucker punched me. I like you better in your old clothes. You were my pal in those clothes." His face bloomed into a dusky rose. "Sometimes I look at a girl and think she's hot. Then I look at some guys and.... You were always safe. Now I can't look at my best friend without wanting –"

Sid couldn't stop staring. Shock continued to reverberate, scattering her thoughts. Taylor couldn't have surprised her more if he'd sprouted a dragon wings and a tail.

His expression closed like a shuttered window. "Forget it. You don't want to know my problems. All you care about is getting in the band." Taylor let the bike lean against his thigh. He took hold of Sid's jean jacket under the collar. "You wanna know what I want from you, Sid?"

Still reeling from his jumbled confession, if that's what it was, Sid nodded.

Taylor shook her. "Smarten up. You're smarter than this. I thought you had limits. I thought you'd walk away if things got too crazy." He released her, pulled a crumpled sheet from inside his leather jacket and shoved it at her. He jammed his helmet on and steered his bike toward the street. He turned the key, flipped the choke out with his toe and gave a vicious jump start. "I guess I was wrong."

"Tay! What is this?" She shook the paper at him.

He glared at her with a mix of anger and hurt, gunned the engine and roared down the street.

The mist increased to a drizzle. Sid frowned at the paper in her hand, opened it and frowned more. The header shouted, *Video Online!* Below it said, *You know what site. Search: french kissing Edwards High.* Sid crumpled the paper in her fist and raced home, slammed the door and darted into the far corner of the living room, beside the archway that opened to the table where James insisted the only Internet computer be kept. The computer was still booted up from when she'd checked email while the spaghetti had boiled. She logged onto the Internet. Sid's fingers quivered as she typed in the search terms.

She muttered, "He wouldn't dare. He wouldn't..."

He had. The first video to come up showed a familiar brick wall, a familiar skirt and top. Sid's gut wrenched. Those jerks had videoed that kiss? She stared at the thumbnail of the video for a minute as her breathing became louder. Finally, she clicked the thumbnail. The video loaded in three blinks.

Her stomach churned as she watched a close up of Rock forcing his tongue down her throat. In the video she groaned, wiggled. She had been trying to free herself but it was hard to tell. Then the picture panned back and she saw his big hand sliding up her thigh to reveal blue lace. "Nice," came a whispered voice-over. The video cut to brick wall and Rock's voice: "She was hot for it. Did you see her squirming for more?"

The view panned left to show Wes's mouth and nose. "And now, for Sidney Crowley's next trick..." The mouth smiled. "Are you ready for it, my friend?"

The camera panned left again to another mouth. "Oh yeah. Bring it on." Clem's voice. The camera panned down to his zipper. Hands flexed and unzipped. The screen went black with "Censored!" slanted diagonally across the screen. Clem must have been the one videoing the kiss. He'd been friendly on Monday to get her to drop her guard and get ammo to use against her. Now he'd teamed up with Wes and Rock to stick it to her.

Was it Wes who had arranged this, or Clem? Did it matter? Bile surged up Sid's throat. She swallowed twice to force it down. She was shaking when she closed the screen. She stared at the computer's background picture of ocean waves as anger rose with far more force than her stomach juices had. She jumped up and kicked over the chair. "Those jerks! Those freaking jerks! I'll kill them!"

"That sounds a little drastic," James said from beside the front closet. "Who has caused such wrath? And why are there shoe tracks across the rug?"

Air was still heaving in and out as Sid gaped at James. The anger was still pushing, still demanding release. It felt like her chest was going to explode. She shouted, "I hate being a girl! It's crap. All of it! The game is made for us to lose and I'm sick of playing it!"

She stormed through the kitchen. James cut her off in front of the door to the basement. "Can we talk about this?"

"No!" She pushed past him and slammed the basement door behind her.

20 | flipping the beat

Some time in the middle of the night a hand shook Sid awake. She was on the green sofa in the drum pit and she was cold.

"Sid?" James asked. "Taylor's mom is on the phone. Do you know where he is?"

Sid tried to wake up, to make sense of the question. It was dumb. Taylor would be in bed. She mumbled, "Sleeping." Hands tucked a quilt over her and she dropped back into oblivion.

"Sid? You need to wake up."

She pried her eyes open. They were dry and itchy and didn't want to work. Neither did her voice. It slurred as she asked, "Wha' time's it?"

"Six o'clock. I'm getting ready to go to work." Sid groaned and tried to roll over. James stopped her. "Sid. This is important. Wake up. Taylor's mom called back. He's in the hospital. I thought you might want a ride over."

"What?" Sid sat up and tried to rub the sleep from her

eyes. All she succeeded in doing was pushing some lumps of mascara in. Her eyes stung. “What do you mean, in the hospital?”

“He had an accident with his motorbike.”

21 | ghost notes

Sid paced up and down the antiseptic hospital corridor, hating the pungent smell, hating that she was here. That Taylor was here. He was in surgery and no one would tell her how he was doing. The two times she had headed toward the surgery waiting room, nurses at a nearby station had looked daggers at her, as if they knew she didn't belong, and she had retreated. And it was fear, raw and stinking, that kept her lingering a few metres away from the waiting room now. She was so afraid *for* Taylor, but even more afraid of what she might be told *about* Taylor.

A familiar figure stepped into the corridor, stretched and rubbed the back of his neck. Mr. Janzen looked like he hadn't slept. Of course he hadn't.

He started to turn away. Suddenly, Sid needed to know. "Mr. Janzen!"

He spun around. "Sid. How long have you been here?"

"Since seven." The big clock in the nurse's station read 9:14.

"Why haven't you joined us?"

Sid used her thumb to point at a scowling nurse. "The wardens. Armed and dangerous."

The nurse's scowl deepened.

Mr. Janzen said, "Could she wait with us, nurse? She's like one of the family."

The nurse sniffed. "I never stopped her from joining you in the first place."

Sid gave Mr. Janzen a shrug. "Her eyes said different." He smiled weakly.

Soon, Sid wasn't sure if being with the family was such a good thing. No one spoke. No one looked at each other. Mrs. Janzen was a bit heavy, and now her rolls bulged, as if she had compressed and was folding in on herself. Despite her dark hair and permanent tan, she looked pale and haggard. Sid had always wondered about that word – *haggard* – and now she knew it looked like an alien was sucking the life out of you, making you shriveled and old.

Taylor's older brother, Miles, was asleep, tilted sideways on the orange molded chair, its arm cutting into his ribs. Sid caught Mr. Janzen watching her. He had the same hazel eyes as Taylor but there wasn't much green about them now. Sid swallowed. "Do you know what happened?" She winced at how loud her voice was over the drone of hospital lighting.

Mr. Janzen looked at his clasped hands. His scalp, kept shaved bald for the last five years, reflected a shiny spot of light that seemed very eye-like. Accusing. His voice was quiet. "The officer said Taylor swerved to avoid a car pulling out of a side street on Jackson Drive. He might have made it..." A sigh spilled onto the polished linoleum. "...but the road was wet and he went into a skid. He hit the car and went flying. His helmet was cracked ..." Mr. Janzen's voice had speeded up but now it came to a crashing halt. Like Taylor had.

Cracked. Sid shivered. That could have been Taylor's head.

"Why did he go riding in the rain?" Mrs. Janzen cried. "Why?"

Miles shifted but didn't wake up. Sid winced. She started for the hallway, stopped. These were her best friend's parents. They deserved the truth. "It was my fault."

Taylor's parents stared at her. Sid forced the words out. "He was pushing his bike into the garage. I stopped him. We argued. He was really angry and took off on his bike."

Mr. Janzen cleared his throat. "What did you argue about?"

"Does it make a difference now? I'm really sorry." She walked out. After trying all morning to find the courage to join them, she couldn't stay, couldn't bear their looks of curiosity or pity. She knew them well enough to know they'd refuse to blame her. But they'd be wrong. If she hadn't started this whole reinvention plan, none of this would have happened.

Reinvent herself. What a laugh. Everything she'd done had backfired. And this was the worst part of it. Taylor in surgery, getting pins to hold his leg together. And James had said something about a broken arm and stitches on his chin.

They hadn't even been able to send him into surgery until this morning because they were worried about a concussion.

The phrase she'd heard when James had dropped her off at the hospital was "lucky to be alive." That was just supposed to be for people in movies, not real people. Not people she knew.

Not Taylor.

Sid charged into a bathroom, splashed water on her face, and studied a reflection that looked battered. Other than the haircut, it looked remarkably like the old Sid, the one that Taylor had said he wanted back. The only "new look" part of her was her jeans, the same pair from yesterday. The Dragonforce shirt was a lie – she didn't feel like a force of any kind, certainly not dragonly. She felt like a timid rabbit, quivering in the corner while she waited through the worst day of her entire life. Even Wes the jerk couldn't match today for making her feel miserable.

She retreated to the cafeteria, got a muffin and a large coffee and found an empty table off to the side, partially behind the fingered fronds of a two-metre tall tropical plant. She emptied three creamers and three sugars into the coffee and stirred. Finally she took a sip. Winced. Took another. This was vile. What did James like about it?

Two-thirds of the way through the cup of coffee, Sid's nerves started buzzing and her fingers vibrated. She held up her hand and watched. *This* is what coffee did to a person? Weird. How could anyone even drive safely when they were this high?

Someone sat down. Sid's head twitched to the left. Mr.

Brock pointed. "You might want to eat that muffin, especially if you aren't used to drinking coffee."

Sid dropped her hand to the table. "Am I that obvious?"

He smiled. "You're looking a little buzzed." He took a sip from his silver travel mug.

Sid bit into her muffin. When she'd chewed and swallowed, she said, "Aren't you supposed to be at school?"

"Your dad called to let us know what was happening so I decided to come down and see how you're doing."

Tears suddenly welled up. "What do you care?"

"I care."

"You're paid to care. You don't. Not really."

"Actually, most counsellors care a great deal. We have a very high burnout rate because a lot of us can't leave our cases at the office. We worry and wonder and lose sleep."

"So I'm a case."

"That's only a term, Sid. Call yourself my patient if you want, though that sounds way too doctorly. Client, maybe. You're a student I've been asked to keep an eye on."

"So do you ever lose sleep over me?"

Brock sipped his coffee and adjusted his trendy glasses. He leaned back, opened his suede jacket and slid a hand into the pocket of his green jeans. All the time he studied her, as if deciding how much to say. "Yes. I have lost a bit of sleep thinking about you."

"Good." He raised his eyebrows. Sid picked up her muffin. "Makes me feel like I'm getting my money's worth."

He chuckled. "Doesn't take much to get value for nothing.

How is Taylor doing?"

"He's in surgery." Sid peeled the paper off the muffin. She pinched off a piece, dropped it on the paper, pinched off another bit, and squished it between her thumb and index finger.

"So how are you doing, Sidney?" She didn't reply. Brock said, "Scared?"

She nodded.

"That's pretty normal."

"Doesn't feel normal. Feels like shit."

"Like I said. Normal."

Sid snorted. "What's normal anyway?"

"For me?" Brock sipped his coffee. "Normal is any behaviour that falls within a socially acceptable or predictable range."

Sid continued to mangle her muffin. "Yeah? Well, I don't feel acceptable or predictable. The only thing predictable lately is my desire to scream my head off." No reply. Sid looked up. Brock paused in mid-sip and raised his brows in a "please continue" kind of way. He'd like that. She lowered her head and began to nibble the bits of muffin. Her head was still buzzing. It didn't help that the noise in the cafeteria, the talking and humming lights and echoing clinks, all sounded like one giant buzz.

"I'd like to keep you company for a while," Brock finally said.

She shrugged.

"I'll be quiet if you want. Unless there's something you

want to talk about..."

Sid peered at him. Concern was stamped all over his face. He knew about the video. *Shitshitshitshitshit.* She kept her head down and ate the rest of her muffin in silence. Then she said, "I think you should go."

"I think I should stay." He sipped more coffee. Very controlled. Annoyingly comfortable when Sid was squirming inside. He leaned forward. "Why don't you tell me..." Sid winced, waiting for the words that would cut her into pieces. "About Taylor."

"What?"

"Tell me how you met. How you became friends. Whatever you want."

"Just Taylor?"

"Unless you want to string me along with more stories about how your mother's leaving is still traumatizing you." He gave her a knowing but amused smile.

He knew she'd lied and hadn't called her on it? Somehow that made her like him a little more. Sid narrowed her eyes. "Was that stuff about losing sleep just BS to get my guard down or did you really mean it?"

He sighed. "Unfortunately I really meant it. I get up and journal whatever I'm worrying about. I can show you the log dates on my laptop if you want." He pointed down at the soft-sided briefcase on the floor by his feet. Sid hadn't noticed it before.

She shook her head. "I'll believe you."

His response was dry. "Why, thank you. Do you want to

tell me about Taylor?"

"Yeah."

Two hours later, Taylor's brother, Miles, found them. "Sid, Taylor's out of surgery. Mom and Dad said you could come up for a few minutes if you want." Miles grimaced. "He doesn't look very good right now. In ICU, tubes everywhere. But if you want, I'll show you..."

Sid dropped the crossword puzzle book Brock had lent her – even the easy puzzles were enough to give her a headache – and jumped up. "I do want. That's why I've been here all morning." She considered Brock. "Want to come? In case I need back up or something?"

He nodded, gathered some papers he'd been reading, stuffed them and the puzzle book into an outer pocket of his briefcase. He offered his hand to Miles. "Paul Brock. School counsellor. I was just keeping Sidney company."

Miles shook hands, gave Sid an odd look and walked off. She hurried to keep pace. They got to the ICU and Miles told the nurses who she was. Five minutes, they said. Brock accompanied her to the door where she hesitated. She tapped her thigh, not wanting to see what was beyond that door.

"I need to head back to school soon, but I can go in with you if you want," Brock said.

Sid started. "No. But if you hear a thud that'll be me hitting the floor. You can scrape me up."

"I'll ask the nurses if they have any shovels."

Sid tried to smile. She took a breath and sidled into the room, back to the wall. The person on the bed was hidden by tubes and bandages. A high frame and a sling suspended the right leg in the air. She pushed away from the wall and inched closer. The head was turned the other way so she circled the bed to get a better look. Miles had said he looked bad and the nurses had said this was his room, but Sid had, deep inside, hoped that they'd all been lying. That Taylor was fine. She gasped when she got a good look at his face.

The bruises and bandages immediately blurred as tears threatened to escape. She wiped them away and blinked rapidly so no more could take their place. Taylor's eyes were closed. She had wanted to look into them and see that everything was going to be okay.

How could it be okay when this was her fault?

22 | bridge to the solo

Sid had found it easy to blend in. She haunted the halls of the hospital, slipped in and out of rooms filled with people waiting for life to resume and fearing it might not. So many faces looked as lost as Sid felt, intimidated by the walls and ceilings and antiseptic air pressing in on them, by the nurses and doctors in their sanitized uniforms tossing incomprehensible words around like they were in some kind of obscure spelling bee. The hum and drone of machines and lights made the building feel alive. Somehow malevolent.

Time and again she returned to Taylor's room, hoping he would be awake, hoping she could look into his eyes. If one of the family members was in the room, she returned to her ghostly wanderings. If Taylor was alone, which wasn't often, she would go in. He was never awake.

The nurses were silent. She was lucky they let her in the room, which they did only on Taylor's parents' okay. She wasn't family and Taylor's information was *for their eyes only.* She could have asked his parents but was afraid they'd press to know more about what happened before the accident.

To feel something besides numbness or pain, Sid went to the maternity ward and peered through the glass of the nursery at the few babies not in their mothers' rooms. She'd never been one to coo over babies so she returned to Taylor's room. It was empty.

Panic slammed into her. She had to grab the door frame to stay on her feet. Air huffed out in rapid bursts. A hand clamped onto her shoulder and she jumped.

"Hey, Sid," Miles said. "We thought you had gone home."

"N-no. Where's..." A feeling of doom lingered as Sid watched Miles cross the room and open the night table's drawer. He removed a watch. Taylor's watch. Sid eyed it with a detached kind of horror.

Miles retraced his steps. "They've moved Tay to the surgical ward. Said he's stable now."

Air hissed out. She gave him a wobbly smile. "Yeah. Sure. Where else would he be?"

Miles paused. "Are you okay? You look really pale."

Sid swallowed. She pointed at the ceiling. "Fluorescent lights do that to me."

They walked from the room. "Come on. He was awake but only for a minute or two. Maybe he'll wake up for you."

"Is he..." Sid wanted to say, *going to be okay.* "Is he in a lot of pain?"

"Nah. He's so drugged up he doesn't know where he is. But he'll hurt when it wears off."

Miles poked the elevator's up button and crossed his arms.

Sid copied the pose. She hadn't realized she was shivering. What was it about hospitals that they kept the temperature so low? Were they saving money, or killing germs by freezing them?

When they stepped into the elevator, Sid said, "How're your folks doing?"

"Pretty shook up. Hell, I am, too." He scowled at the digital floor indicator above the door. "Taylor's a klutz. What was Dad thinking, letting him get a bike?"

The door opened. Sid stepped out behind Miles and grabbed his wrist to turn him around. "It wasn't like that, Miles. Tay's different when he's on his bike. Smooth. He's a good driver."

"You rode with him?"

She nodded. That first ride came to mind, how they'd soared around the curves on Jackson Drive – the place he'd had his accident. That drive had taught her why he loved riding. How free it felt. Miles looked at her in a sad and thoughtful way. Unexpected venom shot through his voice. "I hope he's never stupid enough to get on one of those death machines again."

Sid flinched. That was like saying he hoped a wounded eagle never flew again. She whispered, "You never saw him ride. It was beautiful."

"So is a bonfire. That doesn't mean you stick your hand in it." Miles strode down the hallway.

Sid followed, wondering if Taylor would ride again. Maybe this would change his mind about bikes. Would he still want to become a motorcycle mechanic? Miles was waiting by the third door past the nurses' station. He waved for her to go in.

Mr. and Mrs. Janzen were sitting on either side of Taylor's bed. They both looked when she walked in. Mr. Janzen stood. "Sid, I was wondering if you were still around. Would you like to sit with Taylor while we go to the cafeteria for a bite to eat?"

She nodded, then blurted, "Will he be okay?"

"Yes. But it will be a long road to recovery. Even getting out of the hospital will take some time. We're just glad he's still with us."

Mrs. Janzen rose. Her eyes were bloodshot, her face blotchy. "Taylor's lucky to have such a good friend." She gave Sid a squishy hug and sniffled like she was going to start crying. Sid tensed, no longer used to hugs. Mrs. Janzen released her and patted her cheek. As he passed her, Mr. Janzen ruffled her hair like he used to do when she was younger.

They left her alone with Taylor. The pale yellow room should have been cheerful but somehow managed to be dreary. Maybe it was the tinted windows. Or the machines on either side of the bed that were hooked to her best friend, monitoring him, feeding him, medicating him and whatever else.

Sid edged around the bed and perched on a chair by the window. Taylor's face was turned toward her. It was dark with bruises. Except for fingertips and toes, his whole right side seemed to be either casted or bandaged. His left arm, closer to Sid, had needles and tubes attached like transparent, parasitic snakes. She reached out in slow motion and touched his left fingers.

"I'd do anything to take it back, Tay. All of it. Starting with going to that party."

One of the machines beeped, then resumed ticking.

"Well...except meeting Brad. I think I would've met him anyway because of the wedding. I never got the chance to tell you about him. He's a bit of a geek, but I'm kind of weird, too, so..." She sighed, laid her forearm along the bed's guardrail and rested her chin on her hand. She hated not having Taylor to talk to, and talking to an unconscious Taylor wasn't much of an improvement. She closed her eyes for a few moments. James would be getting off work soon and would be arriving to take her home. She wasn't doing anything useful here but didn't want to go. Even the thought of letting loose on the drums didn't appeal much right now.

She looked up to see Taylor watching her. But his eyes were unfocused, almost crossed, and were looking more through her than at her. She licked dry lips. "Hey, Tay."

A blink. "Shid. Gonna roasht pigtails wit me? Run wit da bananas in da ice tea."

Sid's mouth opened. Nothing came out. She tried again. "Sounds like a great party, Tay."

"Pardy. Wit brads an' giant shkunks." His eyelids drooped. "Dancshing. Bikesh flyin.'"

He was gone again. Not that he'd been here. Roast pigtails? Running bananas? Flying bikes was the only thing that made sense. Some part of him must remember the accident. What had it felt like? Hitting the ground and crumpling the way a tin can does when you step on it.

The pressure of tears started to build. Sid clenched her jaw, refusing to cry. The feeling subsided and Sid settled in to watching, hoping to look into Taylor's eyes when they were clear and focused. She needed him to release her. To forgive her. She scanned his broken form and knew she wasn't going to forgive herself any time soon. If ever.

When James picked her up and took her home, she played her drums until she was dripping sweat and her wrists and forearms were screaming in pain. She knew she was being stupid, but she only stopped when a cramp snapped into her kick drum leg like a bear trap. She fell off the throne and writhed on the floor.

"Ow, ow, ow, ow!" The chant of agony changed into a drawn out wail.

James thundered down the stairs. When he figured out what was wrong, he massaged Sid's calf until the cramp eased a little. He helped her up. "Let's get you to bed. You need to get a good sleep. You'll have lots of homework to catch up on at school."

Sid tried to put weight on her leg. It recoiled in pain. She hissed and let James help her up the stairs. "Not going to school."

"Oh? Where are you going?"

"Hospital."

"There's nothing you can do there, Sid."

James released her and she hobbled toward the hallway. She leaned against the wall. "You can give me permission to miss school or I can skip."

"You've gotten a little too used to getting your own way all the time."

She shrugged. "Devin's at college. Thanks to that promotion, you're *always* working. Who's been around to tell me different?"

He sighed. "You're right, of course. Time like this I wish you had a mother..."

"Well I don't. Just drop that, Dad. Please. And it wouldn't make any difference if I did. I'm still spending tomorrow with Taylor."

23 | buzz roll

Like the previous morning, Mr. Brock found Sid in the hospital's cafeteria, at the same table attempting to wake up with coffee. She hadn't slept very well. Variations of motorcycle crashes kept waking her up. Except in her dreams she'd been driving, Taylor hanging onto her and shouting instructions. "Watch out for that semi!" "Stay away from that broken guardrail!" But whatever he'd told her to avoid was the very thing she'd swerved toward.

Brock looked disgustingly wide awake and almost cheerful. He dropped a thick plastic bag on the chair beside her. "I thought you might come here again today so I took the liberty of collecting your homework from your teachers yesterday afternoon, just in case." He set his Greenpeace travel mug on the table and unbuttoned his casual navy jacket. His patterned shirt looked vaguely Hawaiian, blurred flowery shapes matching his tan cargo pants. He settled his left ankle on his right knee and waited, as if expecting her to thank him.

Sid sipped her coffee and winced. "Does your wife help you dress?"

"No. Why do you ask?"

"I don't know. You always blend so well. A lot of guy teachers don't dress so carefully. A lot of the time they're very...wrinkled." Like she was this morning. Before Heather's makeover she wouldn't have noticed a few wrinkles. Proof that girl was a bad influence.

"I'm not a teacher."

"Yeah. Forgot. You're a fetcher of homework."

"Among other things."

Sid had decided to try toast this morning. It was already cold and she hadn't taken one bite. She opened a grape jelly packet and spread it so thin that one square was enough for all four halves. She took a bite and watched Brock watch her. It was starting to bug her how he always did that. She forced cheerfulness into her voice as she said, "Lose any sleep last night?"

"Not really."

She muttered, "That makes one of us."

He reached for his coffee. "It's tough to sleep when someone you care about is hurt."

"How would you know?"

"My dad died a few years ago. Cancer. I lost a lot of sleep for six months or so."

"Oh." Sid frowned into her coffee. "I wish you wouldn't keep coming here."

"We have things we need to talk about."

"No."

"You can't avoid..."

"No." Sid raised her eyes and met Brock's earnest gaze. "I don't care about anything right now except Taylor. Not homework. Nothing." She formed a circle with her thumb and forefinger. "Not what I look like. Not what anyone is saying about me. Not what you think of me. Nothing."

"Fair enough. But problems don't go away because you avoid them. Sometimes the opposite happens and they get bigger, harder to deal with."

Sid didn't see how things could get much worse, especially at school. "I'll take my chances."

Brock stood and drank down some coffee. "You might be interested to know that members of a certain band were suspended over a video incident that apparently happened on school grounds."

Sid had been reaching for her Styrofoam coffee cup. Horror bubbled up as Brock spoke and she snatched her hand back. It brushed the cup. Coffee splashed across Sid's toast. She jumped up and back, avoiding most of the mess.

"You think that's going to help?" Her voice, shrill and louder than she'd realized, drew the attention of people around them. She dropped into a harsh whisper. "They are the coolest guys in school. I won't be able to show my face there again."

"Were we talking about something that involves you? Are you feeling like talking now?"

"You know, I was starting to like you. But now you sound

like a teacher. Or a cop." Sid grabbed the bag of homework. "Stay away from me." She left the cafeteria without looking back.

The waiting area on the surgical ward was empty. Sid curled into a chair beside a bank of windows and watched puffball clouds scud across the sky. She needed a plan. *Drum roll.* No sudden insights came to mind. Just a big mess. Taylor had asked her how much she was willing to give up to get what she wanted. It seemed to her she'd given up everything and had nothing to show for it. How had that happened, when she'd supposedly had it all under control?

All she wanted to be was a drummer girl. Well, maybe she wouldn't mind being a certain math geek's girlfriend. Sid sat up with a gasp. Brad. What if he found out about the video? She sank back, trying to not consider the possibility. But between that and wanting – needing – to talk to Taylor, her stomach was a churning, foaming pit of acid.

Don't ever think things can't get worse, she chastised herself. Things could always get worse.

24 | paradiddle in the fourth beat

Sid got to see Taylor twice on Saturday. The first time, he had woken up but was really groggy. His parents had told her that his hallucinations on Thursday had caused the doctor to change his medication. Regardless, there were some serious drugs flowing in his bloodstream. The second time, she'd sat with him for over an hour, but he hadn't once cracked open an eyelid.

Sunday morning was more of the same. In the afternoon, James dragged her home to spend a few hours doing the homework from the previous week. Brock had phoned both days, to check in, he'd said, but had missed her so had just left bland "hang in there" messages. And Monday, James was adamant: she was going to school. He was actually going into work late so he could drive her there. It felt like having a police escort.

Sid slipped on a pair of her old baggy jeans and discovered she actually preferred her new ones. Snug, yes, but they had something in them that made them a bit stretchy. So she changed jeans, but decided on an album T-shirt. Metallica's *Ride the Lightning,* with its electrocuted skeleton on the back, seemed graphically appropriate this morning. She did the ultra-light version from Heather's makeup instructions, ran a comb through her hair and met James by the front door.

He had the car out of the garage and ready to go. He glanced at his watch, motioned Sid to move, and ate up the distance to the car with long strides. Sid got into the back seat. James gave her an odd look but said nothing. At the school, he twisted and gave her a lukewarm parental frown. "Well?"

Didn't he understand how much she wanted to be at the hospital? How much she dreaded school? How could he when she hadn't told him anything? Sid settled deeper into the seat and, with a flick of her wrist, said, "Home, James."

"Sidney..."

She sighed dramatically. "Sorry. I've always wanted to say that."

"School. Now."

"You have no idea what a den of horrors you're sending me into. Have you been in a high school recently?" Sid hoped for a quirk of lips. She got a blank stare. Flippancy was not working.

"Out."

"Yeah. Whatever. See you around, James." She slammed the door behind her.

Mr. Franklin was on supervision in the front entrance. She ignored him when he greeted her and speed-walked to her locker. She stowed her gear and headed for the library wing. Just before it she changed course and took the nearest exit.

With a sickening lurch in her gut, she realized she was standing beside the spot where the video had been made. Had Clem been the one with a camera? Like she could've noticed anything with Rock almost smothering her. Gurgling sounds rose from her stomach. She pulled a roll of antacid tablets out of her pocket that she'd snatched from beside the phone. James had them scattered all over the house; he'd never miss one. Was she getting an ulcer now?

"Hey," said a male voice from right behind her.

Sid spun and backed away. A guy who looked familiar followed her. Then she remembered: carpentry class, the guy who was in love with using the lathe. "Simon. What's up?"

"I thought it was you. Saw your vid." He scratched at a pair of zits on his cheek. Nice cheekbones; bad skin. "Thought we could have some fun."

Worse attitude. Sid shook her head for emphasis. "You thought wrong."

"What? You only go for musicians?"

"Didn't your mother ever teach you to not believe everything you see on the Internet?" Sid's heel bumped a ridge of grass. She almost tripped.

Simon used the opportunity to grab her. Without thinking, Sid brought her knee up hard and fast. She felt it sink into soft flesh. Simon dropped like a hammer knocked off a roof. He clutched his groin and groaned; his eye balls almost rolled up into their sockets. Sid had never seen that before.

Part of her mind was instantly curious. But the rest of her was already moving, across the field, off school grounds and to a bus stop two blocks away.

It took her forty minutes to get to the hospital. As she was walking down the sidewalk from the bus stop toward the main entrance, she saw Mr. Brock approaching from the parking lot. She slipped behind the nearest pedestrian, a heavy-set, grey-haired woman in a flowered dress, with tensor bandages winding around her legs and a cane that looked to be wrapped in leather. Brock let someone go through the hospital's automatic doors ahead of him and glanced around. Sid was sure he was looking for her. He disappeared inside.

The woman she was shadowing had a bag of groceries. Sid stepped up and offered to carry the brown paper sack for her. The woman looked immediately suspicious, but Sid gave her best smile and explained how her friend had been in a motorcycle accident but visiting hours hadn't started yet so it would be a huge favour to give her something to do until she could go up to his room.

"I suppose," the woman finally said. "But if you try to run, I'll use this cane. I've tripped up would-be thieves before and I'll do it again."

"I believe you. That's one tough-looking cane."

The woman snorted, pointed with the cane to the high-rise a block away and said that was their destination. "I'm delivering a few items to a friend who can't get out very well."

What Sid could have walked in three minutes took them almost ten. The woman didn't seem frail, just slow. She wasn't talkative. When they reached the apartment building, the woman held her hand out for the bag.

"I can take it up if you want."

"So you can find out the unit number of a helpless woman? No sirree, Bob. You can consider yourself thanked and move on." As Sid shifted the bag to her, she narrowed her pale eyes. "Why aren't you in school? You look of an age you should be in school."

Sid hesitated. "My friend really was in a motorcycle accident. I'm skipping so I see him."

The woman huffed. "Don't you be stupid enough to drop out. That's what I did. Spent my life as a waitress and got the varicose veins to prove it." With that she entered the high-rise.

Sid watched through the glass doors until the woman got on the elevator. She lingered as long as she dared, then walked slowly back to the hospital. Would Brock be waiting to ambush her? She imagined dropping him the way she'd dropped Simon. Maybe not. For one thing, she didn't think he'd ever actually touch her. For another, she still sort of liked him, even with that shock tactic he'd tried to use on her on Friday.

Moving through the building like she was in a third-rate spy movie slowed Sid down even more. She browsed in the gift shop while casing the area near the elevator. When it was clear, she darted over, pressed the button and a scene flashed through her mind, of the elevator opening and Brock standing right there. She took the stairs.

On the third floor landing she peered through the narrow window at the slice of hallway she could see. Voices in the stairwell above her pushed her into action. She could feel her blood thundering in rapid flams. *Da-doom. Da-doom.* No sign of anyone but staff. Sid started toward Taylor's room. She was almost there when she heard Mr. Janzen's voice. She paused mid-step, straining to hear the reply. It was Brock. She ducked into the closest room and hid behind the open door. A man was asleep a few steps away, hooked to a machine that wheezed like it was breathing for him. Brock's voice was louder now. Sid held her breath, heartbeat still racing. *Calm down,* she told herself. *I'm not a criminal.*

Brock was saying, "...appreciate it. And I hope Taylor recovers quickly." His footsteps receded down the hall.

Sid gave it a minute and eased out from her hiding place. Brock was nowhere in sight so she walked into Taylor's room to see Mr. Janzen at the window, looking down at the street. He must have seen movement in the glass because he turned before she was two steps into the room.

"Hi, Sidney," he said. "You just missed that nice Mr. Brock."

"Yeah, I know."

His brow wrinkled and cleared in three beats. "Wanted to miss him, did you? So he was telling it straight when he said you were skipping class?"

Sid nodded. "You going to turn me in?"

"Should I? He asked me to call him if you showed up. He was certain you'd be here and seemed pretty worried that you weren't. Didn't say anything about getting you back to class." He winked. "You should be safe now. He said he couldn't stay."

Sid released a breath she didn't know she'd been holding.

"I'd like to call him, though, set his mind at ease." He held up a piece of paper that probably had a phone number on it.

"I don't want to go back. I want to stay with Tay."

"Understood. I'll call your dad so he knows what's up, then I'll call this Brock fellow."

Sid gave a short nod.

"Good. I have to leave the building to turn on my cell, so why don't you sit with Taylor? His mom and brother are having a coffee break at the shop across the street."

He left and Sid took his sentry position by the window, though she kept her back to it and her eye on Taylor. No sign of improvement. His bruises were more vivid – they looked like they'd been coloured by a five-year-old with garish crayons. They matched the balloon bouquet floating above the wheeled bed tray. Sid looked at the card. *From the staff and students at Edwards High.* The balloons looked fresh; her bet was that Brock had bought them in the gift shop this morning.

She sat beside the bed and slipped her hand through the rails to cup her fingers under Taylor's left hand. His fingers lay limp against hers. She stared at the hand for a long time – it was the only part of him she could see that looked normal. A nurse bustled in, checked the drips, took Taylor's pulse and made a few notes, then left, all without looking at Sid. *I'm invisible,* she thought.

The fingers twitched. Sid's head jerked up. Taylor's eyes were open, barely, and he was looking at her. Better yet, he was *seeing* her. Sid offered a smile. "Hey. Welcome back."

His gaze down drifted from her face and she thought he was going back to sleep, but it rose again. "Hey, yourself." His voice was a thin rasp. "You're back, too."

Sid glanced down at her Metallica shirt. "Yeah, well. Don't get used to it. I don't think I can go back to all baggy all the time."

His breathing grated and the corner of one eye flinched. Sid had no idea if that was a response to what she'd said or something else. She scooted the chair as close as she could get it and cradled his hand in both of hers. "Tay, please tell me you didn't believe that video."

His eye twitched again, more like a series of tiny spasms. "Knew it...after I'd cleared my head with a ride. Last thing... remember wanting to get home, call you."

Relief surged through Sid. She gave his hand a squeeze. "I'm sorry we argued, Tay. This is all my fault." He said nothing, just breathed like it was taking a lot of effort. She continued, "My great plan hasn't worked out so well. And I've missed talking to you, you stupid jerk."

His mouth almost lifted but then sagged into a grimace.

"Did I ruin things between us, Tay? I mean, will you ever be able to think of me as your friend again? I don't know what I'll do if you can't. You've been my best friend for years.

Almost my only friend, except maybe for Narain, but he puts up with me because of you, mostly." Sid clamped her mouth shut. She was spewing like a busted fire hydrant.

"Didn't think you'd want to be friends after, after what I said," Taylor whispered. "You looked...horrified."

"I was surprised, that's for sure. You've got to know nothing's going to stop me wanting to be your friend. We've got history. You're stuck with me for life, if you can stand to be around me. I'm not really very hot at all." The corner of Taylor's mouth rose. Sid smiled. "You were a little tough on me, though. You were pissed off, I guess. I don't blame you because I was choked when I saw the video. I'm sure Wes set that up. Or Clem got him to. I wanted to kill them both. It's still tempting. Makes me sick to think I was that stupid."

"Why?"

Sid hesitated. It looked like Taylor was taking every bit of strength he had to listen. And it looked like he was in a lot of pain. "Are you okay? Should I call a nurse?"

"Not yet. Tell..."

So Sid told him about Wes leading her into the trap and how she'd gotten backed up against the wall by Rocklin. "Thanks to the editing job on that video, Wes probably has the drummer gig sewed up." Sid couldn't believe she'd just said that. Could a part of her still want to join TFD? Rocklin had forced a kiss on her and told her to get lost. She didn't want to hang around jerks like that. "As a bonus, his hassling campaign will be picked up by other guys." She told him about having to knee Simon that morning when she'd been leaving the school.

His eyebrows hung low, obscuring his eyes. His fingers had curled into a hot fist in the cocoon of her hands. But it was his breathing that alarmed Sid. It had grown louder, more irregular. She placed Taylor's hand on the bed and darted to the door.

"Nurse? " she called loudly. A woman at the nursing station raised her head. "I think Tay needs some medicine or something."

The nurse was instantly on the move. Her rubbed soled shoes squeaked on the gleaming linoleum. As she passed Sid who had pressed herself against the door frame, she said, "There is a call button at the bed. Shouting can upset our other patients."

She fussed around Taylor for a few minutes, adjusted some drips, tucked and straightened his bedding, took his pulse again. Sid had eased toward the bed and now stood at its foot.

The nurse skewered Sid with a sharp glare. "Visiting is very tiring for someone in his condition. His medication has been cut back to every four hours and he isn't due for more yet. It's easier to control pain when you're resting peacefully. You should leave now and let him do that."

Sid's fingers tapped against her thigh in a rapid paradiddle rhythm. "I won't talk, okay? I promised Mr. Janzen I'd stay 'til they got back."

The nurse gave her a skeptical glance and double-checked the drips. She paused by Sid on her way out. "Not a word." She walked out of the room. Crisply. Without a backward glance.

Sid inched around to Taylor's left side. She was going to whisper something to him about the nurse being one tough bag, but his eyes were already starting to close. Before they did he managed a barely audible whisper. "Be you."

The Janzens gave Sid another bedside shift in the afternoon. He slept. She held his hand and tried to decide if their short conversation meant that Taylor forgave her. He hadn't actually said so, but at least they were talking. As for the rest, she guessed Taylor couldn't or hadn't decided if he preferred girls or guys. She didn't much care. He was still Taylor; she was still Sid. And if she had anything to say about it, they were still friends.

When the Janzens relieved her, Sid made her way home on the bus. She walked from the bus stop, head down, shoulders slumped, every step an effort. The image of Taylor, tethered in his bed by tubes and slings, pulsed in her mind, accompanied by the monotonous beat – *beep, beep* – of a hospital monitor.

Jean-clad legs and feet blocked the front step. Sid raised her head. "Brad? What are you doing here?" It came out wrong: accusatory when she was relieved. Surprised, but relieved.

"Is it true?" He pushed his glasses up his nose and stared.

A bass drum started booming in her stomach. "What?"

"That you and your boyfriend had a fight, and that's the only reason you even looked at me at the wedding." Brad joined her on the sidewalk. "That he had some kind of accident and you've gone running back to him."

"Taylor's a friend. That's all he's ever been, Brad. I just spent all day at the hospital, watching my best friend, bruised and broken and eaten up with pain – and you think..."

Jumbled emotions paraded across Brad's face. His eyebrows lowered to hide behind his glasses. "So what I heard was a lie? And I shouldn't believe that there's a video with you Frenching with some band guys...and other things."

"Shit." Had it gone viral that fast?

Brad made a disgusted noise.

Sid grabbed Brad's forearm. "I was set up. And I swear I didn't do any *other things.* Please say you believe me."

"Why? Because we have such a long and trusting relationship?"

"No! Because..." James pulled into the driveway, beside Brad's jeep which she hadn't even noticed before. From behind the wheel he watched them and radiated fury. "Look. Heather must have told you all those lies. Believe me because I like you. Has Heather *ever* been nice to you, Brad? Even once? Was she being nice to you when she told you all that crap?"

For a second he looked like he wanted to believe her. Then he pulled free and walked away, brushing by James without a word.

James blocked her view, scowling as they both listened to the jeep's engine whine in reverse, then rev as it accelerated down the street. "Do you mind explaining to me what he was doing here when I thought you were at the hospital?"

"Yes, I mind. I mind a lot."

25 | one hand crossover

Jazz sashayed through Sid's headphones and into her fingertips. She was using brushes instead of sticks, working to control the flow so her drumming slid under the music wafting through her mind and buoyed it up instead of drowning it. She started the song over again, for the umpteenth time, then the thought of those jerks flung her into an angry fill, a crash of bass and cymbals. She threw down the brushes – they didn't work at all for venting.

Sid found a Rush song on her iPod and lay on the rug, listening to it over and over as she worked out drum tabs for it, then returned to the drums and attempted to follow Neil Peart's lead. He was a tough one to keep up with. On the sixth go through, when she was starting to feel like she was making some headway, movement on the stairs made her pause. She didn't look, decided to keep going and played the song a seventh time before she let James interrupt her. He was being very patient.

When the song finished, she laid her sticks on the snare

and removed her headphones.

Brock sat on the third step up, wearing a red golf shirt and jeans with a hole in one knee. She'd never seen him in such casual clothes. He clapped slowly. "I have no idea what song you were accompanying, but it sounded good from here."

"'Workin' Them Angels.'"

Brock smiled. "One of the newer Rush CDs. That's a good song."

"You listen to Rush?"

"Sometimes. They've been around for a long time." He leaned against the wall and propped one foot on the bottom step. "So are you?"

"What?"

"Working them angels? You know, your guardian angels?"

"If I ever had any, they've moved on to an easier gig."

"Tough week."

"Why are you here?"

"Your dad called this morning, pretty choked you were skipping, so I asked him if I could come over this evening. I needed to talk to you anyway."

"Losing sleep?"

"Actually, yes. It took me three cups of coffee to get moving this morning." He didn't change position, but Sid noticed new alertness in his body, as if his casual pose hid his readiness to spring into action. "You need to know what's been happening, Sid. It's getting way bigger than either of us could have predicted."

"I don't know what you're talking about."

"Yes, you do. I need honesty, Sid. And I need you to hear me out. A friend of yours came into my office last Wednesday, forty minutes after class ended. I was packing up to go home."

"Taylor?" No. That would have been around the time they had been arguing, just before he took off on his bike.

"Narain. He was shaking he was so upset. Gave me a copy of a photocopied poster that had been plastered all over the school. So I booted up my laptop and searched out the video. Narain defended you loudly, said that wasn't your style. It certainly looked to me like Rocklin forced his attention on you. And that editing at the end was totally unacceptable. I'm really sorry they subjected you to that, Sidney. I tried to talk to you about it on Friday at the hospital but I'm afraid my approach was a bit heavy-handed. Like a cop, I think you said."

The back of Sid's eyes started to sting. Narain had stood up for her? What a stupid thing to want to cry about. She should be happy. Instead she felt even more miserable. She moved to the sofa and curled up on one end.

Brock crossed the room and sat on the floor at the other end of the sofa. "Is that why Taylor had his accident? Because he was upset about the video?"

Sid nodded. A few tears slipped down her cheeks. She wiped them away with hasty swipes. She hated crying, and in front of someone was the worst. "At first he thought it was true. Yesterday he told me that his ride had cleared his head. Until that car..." More tears. "Shit."

"It's okay, Sid. Tears are a release, not a sign of weakness."

She still gulped them back, forced herself back into a semblance of control. When she felt like she could speak, she said, "Other than my life being shot to pieces, what's so big about this?"

"Isn't that enough?" He rested his forearms on his upraised knees. "I went around and removed any posters I could find. But VP Finning had gotten a hold of one. She called me at home on Wednesday night and it spiraled from there. Those boys were smart enough to keep their faces off camera, but their voices were easy to identify. I really want to say that Rock cracked like a piece of thin shale." He paused.

Was he waiting for Sid to smile at his bad pun? She sniffed loudly and hugged her knees closer. Brock continued, "Han admitted who was involved. All four boys are suspended until Wednesday. There could be further disciplinary action."

"A longer suspension?"

"No, Sidney." Brock shifted so he was facing her. "I mean that VP Finning is furious that this happened on *her watch,* as she put it, and she's pushing this as far as she can. She has called in the police."

26 | right hand lead

Sid gaped at Brock.

He glanced at his watch. "An officer will be showing up any minute to get your statement. We might want to head upstairs. I can stay during the interview if you want."

"Statement?" she squeaked.

"Yes. They've already interviewed all four guys, and got a copy of the video off Wes's computer. They're part of a special liaison unit working with the schools. Mostly they try to educate, but in serious cases like this they will investigate." He stood up and brushed off. "You'll be happy to know that Wes's parents made him take the video down. I have the feeling he might not have Internet privileges for a while."

"But the police?"

"After they get their statement from you, they'll decide how to proceed."

"Meaning?" Sid followed when Brock headed toward the stairs.

He spoke over his shoulder as he ascended. "Meaning they

might want to press charges."

Sid absorbed that thought in silence as they walked into the kitchen. Charges. Did that mean court, a trial? If Wes was the ringleader he might get nailed. He had screwed up her life in so many ways she had lost count. Now...

Something inside gave a victory shout. *Payback time.*

James stood at the sink, back to the room, downing a glass of milk. Sid saw the open bottle of antacid tablets on the counter. Victory burned to ashes in a flash of guilt.

"I had to tell him," Brock whispered. "It should've been you, Sidney. You should've let him know what was happening."

She almost dropped the F-bomb, something she'd promised James she'd never do. He hated that word above all words. She glared at Brock. "Did he see it?"

He shook his head. Sid's relief was short-lived.

The doorbell rang. James turned. "I'll let you get that, Sid, and since you don't seem to want to keep me informed, I'll be in my office."

"Dad..." He strode past her without looking. "Dad!"

He hesitated by his office door. "You're right, Sid. I'm never around for you lately. This promotion has consumed my life and I let my job become more important than my family. But this... I'm sorry. I can't listen to you tell a police officer what you wouldn't tell me. That probably makes me a lousy dad. I think I already was one." He disappeared into his office.

Sid swore in her mind. Her mouth was so dry nothing came out.

Brock said, “Do you want me to stay?”

She nodded. She didn’t want to face this alone.

Brock laid his hand on her shoulder. It was the first time he’d ever touched her. “I like you, Sid. I like your dad. The pair of you need to work out some stuff, but I’m sure you know that. I run a private practise on Tuesday and Thursday evenings and I’d really like to counsel you together. Think about it, okay?”

Sid moistened her lips. “Dad’ll never agree.”

“Actually, he already has, but he’s leaving it up to you.”

Talk about dropping a bomb. Sid frowned at him. “Yes, no, maybe, I’ll think about it.”

“Well, that about covers it. Bad timing, I know. We’ll talk in a week or two.”

Officer Downing was about the same age as Brock, or a few years younger. And female. That made things easier. They sat at the kitchen table and Sid outlined what had happened. The officer wanted to know what had led up to this incident, so Sid found herself having to tell all, starting with the party and the audition and how trying to change her image blew up in her face. On one level it was humiliating, but on another, Sid felt a lead weight lifting. She was finally getting to talk to someone. She almost forgot Brock was there, taking notes in his mind.

When she was done the officer threw another curve ball at her. “You realize, Sidney, that this might be more serious than cyber bullying, as if that weren’t enough.”

“What do you mean?”

“Well, if things happened as you claim, then we’re talking alleged sexual assault.”

Sid gaped at her. “When Brock mentioned charges, I thought he was talking about posting the video on the ‘Net.” She squinted at him. “Did you know about this?”

“I thought it might be a possibility.”

“But...it was just a kiss.”

“No,” the officer said. “You’re talking like it was a peck on the cheek. His tongue was down your throat. A very sexual act. The video clearly shows that. And if it was forced as you allege, that makes it sexual assault, which is very serious. Criminal code. You need to decide if you’re going to press charges.”

Sid was silent as Brock showed the officer out. She tried to wrap her mind around everything that had been said. She drifted to the front entrance.

“Sidney,” Brock said, as he slipped into a jean jacket, “take one more day of grace if you like, but you have to come to school on Wednesday. Without fail.”

That cleared the mist from her thoughts. She bit her lip, then made herself stop and said, “Do you have any idea how crappy that day will be for me?”

“Way crappier than you know.”

“Meaning?”

“I mentioned Officer Downing is part of a police-school liaison team. She and her partner will be talking to the whole student body in an assembly.”

“About the video?” Sid’s voice cracked.

"Yes. And about the lies and manipulation and sexual harassment."

"I have to sit through that? Even if they don't name names, everyone will know it's me."

"I think you should hear it, but I can arrange for you to be backstage."

"And the guys?"

"They'll be there. Right after, the police will meet with them and their parents."

"I still don't see why I have to be there." She forced bravado into her voice, but inside felt sick at the prospect of even accidentally coming face-to-face with those guys. Especially Rocklin. Just thinking of him made her want to gag. The coolest guys around had talked to the police because of her, might be facing charges because of her. What was she supposed to do?

Taylor's accident had given her an excuse to hide from the whole mess, and she realized now that she had done just that. She really wasn't sure she could go through with Wednesday. But she realized that to not go through with it was to face another day just like it when she did return.

"I'm starting to think that dropping out is a better and better idea. Or home schooling."

Brock smiled, unperturbed by the suggestion. "Only if you want to spend your life being afraid, Sidney. And you don't strike me as the type who likes to do that."

"I've been doing it."

"And how do you feel?"

"Like I want to hit something."

Brock laughed. "Pretty normal reaction, I'd say. Make sure you tell your dad what's happening Wednesday. He needs to know. And you've got a lot to think about. I'll leave you to it." He handed her a business card. "If you want to talk, call my cell. Any time. Okay?"

"3 a.m.?"

"I'll probably be awake." He winked and walked out the door.

27 | eighth-note triplets

Tuesday Sid alternated between stewing and doing the homework Brock had so kindly dropped off. In the evening James took her to visit Taylor. James never left the room – part of the grounding he had meted out for skipping school Monday was not being out of sight – and even though Taylor was awake, she never got the chance to catch him up on what was happening. But she didn't need Taylor's advice on this one, anyway. After the day she'd had she'd pretty much decided she wanted the police to throw the book at Wes and the band. More than that, use the book to squash them like the bugs they were.

She'd told Brock she wanted to hit something – now more than ever. She wondered if she should take up boxing.

When they left the hospital, James said he had to stop at Aunt Kathy's. That suited Sid. Heather owed her a few answers. Aunt Kathy answered the door and told Sid to go to Heather's room, that she was doing homework.

Sid tapped on Heather's door and walked in without

waiting for an answer. Her cousin was on the floor, wearing only her panties and bra, and blowing on her fingernails as she read a magazine spread out on the floor. She looked up in total unconcern and returned to her reading.

Sid dropped onto the creamy satin duvet. "*Cosmopolitan?* What class is that for?"

Heather shook her head. "My efforts were so lost on you. Look at yourself. The jeans are fine, but another stupid band shirt. How many of those do you own?"

"Not enough." Sid smiled pleasantly. "I kind of like mixing and matching. You taught me lots of good stuff. But some of the tops you picked out feel too...skanky."

"Oh? I hear that's your new style." Heather said it lightly, as if discussing the merits of yellow jelly beans over green.

Sid slid to the floor with a thud and rested fists on thighs. She tried to keep images of the video out of her head, wishing she'd pocketed another roll of antacids. Her voice was raw. "I was framed." She cleared her throat. "So who did you tell about me and Brad? Because somehow it got to our school."

Heather paused with her brush fanned across her thumb nail. "That little infatuation? You might say you prefer nice over cool, but when that dishy guy came to me and started asking about you I knew you'd changed your mind."

Sid leaned forward and scowled at the makeup ad on the magazine page that lay open. She *had* said that. Nice *was* important to her. That's why she was friends with a couple of nice guys. Why hadn't that counted for her? Had she been temporarily insane, thinking that being in the band was the absolutely, most important thing?

She leaned against the bed and sighed. "With dating, yeah, I like nice. I wish you hadn't told Brad that crap about Taylor being my boyfriend and me going wild because we'd split."

Heather carefully replaced the brush in the nail polish bottle and secured the lid. She twisted to face Sid, her puzzlement written on her face. "I never said that to Brad. Though come to think of it, the second time the dishy guy talked to me, I pointed Brad out to him and he talked to Brad after he left me. Maybe he was eliminating the competition."

She looked and sounded so sincere. Sid tapped her knee harshly. "Hang on. What dishy guy are you talking about?"

Heather blinked rapidly. "How could you not know? He was so intense. Wanted to know everything about you. Wanted to hook up. At least, that's what he said."

"Did he have a name or did he just call himself Dishy Guy?"

"Of course he had a name. It was almost a girl's name. Oh! I remember. Because after he walked away, Coral and I started singing, 'Oh my darling, oh my darling, oh my darling, Clementine'." She giggled. "So, did this Jeff Clementine guy ask you out?"

Clem. Sid's stomach churned and rage thundered in her ears. "That jerkwad. He didn't ask me out. And he won't." He had found out about Brad from Heather and had told him that crap about Taylor and her. Clem had been the driving force behind everything. Sid wanted to drive, too –

her fist into his face. She struggled to relax her fists. To breathe.

Heather interrupted Sid's racetrack of thoughts. "So Coral was practically salivating on Thursday, just had to tell me a rumour about you and a nasty video. I told her no way would you do that." She paused. "I was joking earlier, you know. I didn't teach you to dress skanky. Nothing we bought was at all sleazy. That was just a dig about this video Coral mentioned, which wasn't even there when I checked, by the way. But that's what you meant isn't it? About being framed? The video was real?"

Sid bit the inside of her lip, frowned at Heather's orange nails and nodded. "Clem set it up." *Breathe-2-3-4. Exhale-2-3-4.* He wasn't worth losing her cool over.

Heather lifted her shoulders almost delicately. "If it means anything, I am sorry. I wish now I hadn't talked to him."

Like Heather would not talk to a cute guy. Sid stood. "Sure. Listen. I'm going to let you finish up. Maybe I'll get some fresh air." Clear the stink from her thoughts.

James, Aunt Kathy and Uncle Peter were talking over coffee in the kitchen. Sid paused by the table. "Take it easy on the coffee, Dad. You're past your limit for the day." She glanced at Uncle Peter. "Mind if I go sit on your deck?" He waved his permission.

The deck had three levels. The highest had a hot tub and French doors that led to the master bedroom. The middle and lower decks were dotted with padded chairs and potted plants. Flower beds nestled against all three fences, separated from pristine grass by a brick retaining wall that curved in and out to give the impression of waves. It was beautiful and looked just like Sid's living room: a place where no one lived.

Sid went to the top deck and leaned against the rail. The neighbour to the left had an equally manicured yard, but the one to the right was messy by comparison. The owners were even allowing a few dandelions to invade, which was probably totally against neighbourhood policy. There was a vegetable plot speckled by weeds and half hidden by a lengthening fence shadow, and a chest-high portable pool glowing blue in the evening sun.

While Sid watched, Brad entered the yard pulling a hose. Sid had expected that he lived a few houses away, like Taylor did on her block. Brad tugged the hose to the back of the yard. He plucked a few weeds from the garden, then stood back and turned on the hose's nozzle.

Sid headed to the fence, picking up a chair as she went. She straddled the chair over a clump of green shoots and balanced on its frame as she hoisted herself up. Her elbows hung down into Brad's yard. He hadn't noticed her.

Someone small with a black mop of curly hair, who could only be Brad's sister, opened a back door and yelled at Brad to remind him to water her pumpkins. The girl spotted Sid and stared for a moment, then yelled, "Brad's got a girlfriend!" and ducked back inside.

He startled at that and looked all around. He turned the hose at the same time and a spray of water almost caught Sid. It did get the fence. Brad was facing her now, ears like red flags.

Sid said, "If you step a little closer you can soak me...if that's what you're trying to do."

"What? Oh." Brad released the nozzle trigger and dropped the hose. He advanced toward her warily. Did she look like she might bite? "What are you doing here?"

"Dad came over to see his sister. I'm grounded so was forced to come."

He stood an arm's length away. His head almost came to the top of the fence. "Why grounded?"

"For skipping school on Monday."

"So you could be with your boyfriend."

"Don't start that, Brad." Sid looked both ways, saw no one, jumped so her waist was folded over the top of the fence, swung a leg over and leaped down. She fell by Brad's feet. He made no move to help her up. She brushed herself off and planted her fists against her hips. "Taylor has only ever been my friend. Period."

"You must have a boyfriend. You kiss too good to not have experience."

"Funny, I thought the same thing about you." Surprise claimed his expression. Sid shrugged. "Maybe we just fit when it comes to that."

He considered this for a moment. "And the video thing?"

She sighed and leaned against the fence, then straightened and brushed at her now damp sleeve. "Can I tell you a story? Then I'll go. I promise."

He stood for a full minute, studying her, the fence, the

sky. Finally he motioned toward dry grass, and they both sat. He edged away so they weren't in danger of touching. Sid told him the same thing she'd told the police officer the day before, but in shortened form. It was less painful this time, because she'd done it once, but also because she found Brad so easy to talk to. When she was finished, he sat in silence.

Sid stood and brushed off her backside. Brad stayed where he was, frowning at his hands. Sid crouched back beside him and he looked up. She wanted, more than anything, to give him one last kiss. She leaned forward slightly, stared into his ocean-coloured eyes, wishing she could lose herself in their depths. With a quiet sigh, she said good-bye and walked along the fence to the front gate she'd only just spotted.

With each step she reminded herself, *Don't look back.*

28 | dynamic range

Sid arrived at school at 9:15 and went to Brock's office. He wasn't there, but shortly returned from getting the police officers set up for the 9:30 assembly. He escorted Sid to the backstage area, out of sight of anyone in the auditorium, just minutes before the announcement came for classes to make their way to the assembly. The well-practised drill took less than fifteen minutes.

Sid was deep in shadows when she noticed Brock across the stage in the other wing, showing some adults to chairs. The parents of Wes and the band? Sid pulled out a fresh roll of antacid tablets and popped two into her mouth.

The police officers did their schtick, telling the students about cyber bullying and how easy it was to manipulate information on the Internet, giving all the usual warnings against such behaviour, moving on to how certain types of behaviour qualified as sexual harassment. Sid could hear rustling and could imagine how bored all the students were. Even she was bored.

Then Officer Downing said, "Now we come to the specifics of why we're here. We want to address a case of cyber bullying that happened last week in this school."

Dead silence. Sid sank onto the floor and hugged her knees to her chest. It was hard to hear over the thrumming in her ears and she figured she missed half of what was said as the officers discussed the "case," minus names, its seriousness and possible outcomes. They included a warning that any harassment of the girl involved, or of any girl in a similar manner, could result in charges. The male officer finished off by saying, "You are all over twelve years of age. That means you are all old enough to stand before a judge and be held legally accountable for your actions."

More silence. It stretched and stretched, wrapped around Sid's throat. Squeezed. Needing air, she slipped away. She couldn't leave the school, so she retreated to Brock's office and opened a window. Cheek against the screen, she counted her breaths. Four counts in; four counts out.

They were going to do it. They were going to charge the guys. Yesterday that would've thrilled her. Why didn't she feel happy? Why did she feel her insides tying into endless knots?

Footsteps tramped by the door. Sid glanced and saw the adults who'd been in the other wing filing past Brock's window. She turned her face away, not wanting any of them to look her in the eye. They must be meeting in the staff room. The parents, the guys, the police and, no doubt, Brock. His hand was in all of this.

The door opened. Brock poked his head inside. "I hoped

this is where I'd find you. Thanks for sticking around. I won't be long, Sidney. Stay here."

Sid found a National Geographic DVD about the rain forest and put it in the player-TV combo in the middle of the wall of shelves. She settled into Brock's chair and waited. So far she'd spent the day being invisible, but she was going to have to face people soon. She'd have to walk into class and everyone would stare. She really hated that thought. Rare monkeys and anacondas and piranhas weren't making her feel any better about things.

James walked in. He seemed startled to see her, though the secretary had to have told him where she was. Before she could speak, he blurted, "Listen, Sid. I know you don't want me here, but I'd like to be. I want to know how things turn out. I'll wait outside this office, but I want you to know I'm here. And... I'll support you no matter what happens. Okay?"

"Yeah. Okay, Dad. Ah... Yeah."

He stepped forward as if he might hug her, then sighed and turned away.

"Daddy?" He spun back. Sid stood. "Why don't you hug me any more?"

"You...you're a young woman now, Sid. I thought I was, you know, giving you space. It can get awkward for a dad, having his little girl look and, ah, feel so womanly." He fell silent, slid his foot forward half a step. "Do you...want a hug?"

She closed her eyes and nodded. The next thing she knew familiar arms were wrapping her in a bubble of warmth. Her hands rested against James's chest and his heartbeat pulsed against her palms.

He kissed the top of her head. "I love you. I'm sorry I let my job become more important than you. It isn't." He released her. "Do you want me to stay in here or wait outside?"

She glanced around the small room. Two people made it seem crowded. "I wouldn't mind being alone for a bit. So I can think. Just knowing you're out there is good."

He nodded and left. She was still staring at the door when Brock came in. "Listen, Sid. It isn't quite playing out like I'd thought."

Before she could reply, VP Finning's solid frame filled the doorway. She scowled at Brock. "I want this done and over, Mr. Brock. Just the way we agreed." She left and Brock quietly closed the door, then leaned against it as he faced Sid. "I want you to understand that none of this is my choice. I was forced to agree."

She gave him a questioning look.

"And I want you to understand that I believe what you told Officer Downing. All of it."

"What's going on, Brock?"

He closed his eyes and sighed. "The police won't be pressing charges. They said there isn't enough evidence to support your claims. The video is inconclusive." His eyes flew open. "I disagree with that. I think it's very plain that you were forced. But they don't think it's clear enough to hold up in a court of law. And beyond the video, there is just Rocklin's word against yours. The other boys are supporting him, saying you were willing."

"What? How could they –" Of course they could. Rocklin was their leader, and they'd never desert him. Loyal to the end. "That stinks."

"It does. And it means the police are handing the situation back to the school."

"So what exactly did you and VP Finning agree to?" She quickly amended, "I mean, what did she tell you had to happen?"

"She wants reconciliation. The boys did admit they recorded the kiss and that they posted it without your permission. So they have to apologize to you and that will be the end of it."

"That stinks worse. None of the apologies will be genuine. You know that. So what if I refuse?"

"Then VP Finning told me she will assume that you were in on this little 'video prank,' as she called it, and that it was all for the purposes of advertising Rocklin's band. And she will suspend all of you for the whole week."

"All! Including me?"

Brock nodded. "I protested as strongly as I could. You're the victim here. But she's adamant. The apologies are where it ends so far as the school is concerned."

Sid sat and rested her forearms on Brock's desk. "Fine. Whatever. And I'll laugh in their faces for their fakeness."

"You sound a little angry, Sidney."

"Do I? Where will we be doing this apology crap?"

"VP Finning is letting me handle the actual apologies. We

can do it right here. They'll come in one at a time."

"Oh, good." The thought of it made Sid pop another pair of antacid tablets. "And you?"

"I'll stay beside you if you'll let me."

"Why not? You do strive to be the grand puppet master, after all." He gave her a puzzled look and she blurted, "Did you call my dad?"

"No."

She sank back in the chair, folded her arms and drummed her hidden fingers against her ribs. James had decided to be here without any prompting? That was something she wished she had time to think about. Maybe Brock wasn't manipulating them like she'd thought.

Han came in first. He hadn't had anything to do with the video scam except to watch it unfold, but he sounded truly sorry about that, and pretty disgusted with his friends. Not enough to tell the truth about the forced kiss. Sid couldn't bring herself to laugh.

Clem was belligerent as he explained he'd been in a band where a girl had caused problems and he didn't want one in his band. Ever. No matter how good she played. He grudgingly admitted he and Wes might have stepped over a line in posting the video online.

That was all. Here was the real puppet-master, but he didn't admit to that. Sid was too choked by his attitude to say anything at all.

Clem left and Rocklin walked in with his mother, who looked extremely put out at having to go through this process. Sid turned to Brock and whispered, "Why is she here?"

"She insisted that if I stay, she stays. And there is no way I'm leaving you alone with him, Sid. Just go with it. You're doing great."

Rock also appeared plenty ticked off. Not at Sid, as it turned out. "Wes and Clem set me up. They were the ones who played me, not you. I didn't know about that video. I swear. We were all laughing and joking around after and I said a few stupid things, but that unzipped fly thing? No way. I didn't even know they did that."

Rocklin took a deep breath. "Thing is, you're a great drummer. That's all that should matters. Man, the music *is* all that matters."

Sid's breath froze in her lungs. Was he going to offer her the gig, after everything he'd done? For less than a second the idea appealed to her. Taylor would appreciate the irony. The very thing she'd wanted, offered at last. She licked her bottom lip, and noticed Rocklin follow the gesture with his gaze.

Remembered the feel of his lips, his body crushing hers. The pain. The fear.

Thoughts of Taylor lying in the hospital, of Narain standing up for her, of Brad's kisses, even of Joanne's kindness, spiraled through her mind. No, she didn't want the break Rocklin was about to offer her. Oh, she wanted to get into a band, but on her terms. Not his. Not anyone else's. When she told him Taylor would laugh and say, "I told you so." And she'd reply, "I'm doing what you told me to, Tay. I'm only trying to be me."

But the offer never came. Rocklin only repeated, "You're a great drummer."

"That's your idea of an apology?" Sid shook her head. "Well then, here's my version of an acceptance: I am good and I want you to walk out of here knowing that I'm the best thing that never happened to your band."

He looked a little confused; his mother looked thoroughly insulted. Before the woman could respond, and she looked like she was going to, Brock showed them out.

Minutes later Wes walked in and took the chair she usually occupied. A grim-faced older version of him followed and stood beside the chair. Sid almost rolled her eyes. Great. Another over-protective parent. Brock closed the door and took position beside Sid. Like sides squaring off on a tennis court. A good thing her dad was outside; the room wasn't made for this many people and was really heating up.

"Do it," Mr. Remichuk said. Sid could tell where Wes got his forcefulness.

Wes wrung his hands as if washing them. He definitely had that "caught in the cookie jar" look. Sid wondered if she should suggest he join the drama team. He glanced up, revealing bloodshot eyes, and quickly ducked his head again. "I treated you pretty bad, Sid."

She waited. That was it? That was the big apology?

Mr. Remichuk flicked the back of Wes's hair. Wes flinched. "I... I had no right to hassle you like I did. The, the taunting stuff. And the video..." He rubbed his palms against his thighs. "I had no right... It was..."

He almost sounded sincere. He also sounded like an idiot. Sid decided to help him out. "It was...stupid? Cruel? Did you know I had to fight off a guy with a knee to his balls because of that video? Did you know that this apology might not do anything to stop that kind of jerk? Why *should* I accept your apology, Wesley? For that matter, have you even apologized for basically ruining my life?" He started to stammer. Sid said, "Apologies work better if you look the person in the eye, Wesley."

Wes frowned and lifted his face. "I am sorry, okay, Sid? I mean really sorry. I'm knee-deep in shit because of this –"

"Yeah. That's the most honest thing you've said. You're in trouble so *now* you're sorry. Not because of what you did to me, but because of what's happening to you."

Mr. Remichuk cleared his throat. "Now you listen, young lady –"

"No," Brock said. "This is between them."

Wes gave Brock a look that bordered on thankfulness. "I can't blame you for being angry, Sid. And I wouldn't blame you if you pushed it into court. What we did to you *was* crappy. I knew it then." He stood. "If it means anything, I'd take it back if I could." He walked out. His father followed.

Sweat trickled down the back of Sid's neck. "What did he mean, if I pushed it into court?"

Brock went to the door, whispered something and closed it. He took the student's chair, leaving Sid in his spot. She pulled her legs up against her chest and waited. He said,

"The police explained the possible outcomes to the boys and their parents. There might not be enough evidence to charge Rocklin with sexual assault, but you could sue for defamation of character."

"What do the police think will happen if I do that?"

"They don't get involved in civil suits. Privately they suggested to me that you think very carefully before you take that route. It would be as ugly as a regular trial. And they know you have to walk these halls so they want you to be comfortable with the outcome."

"That band is the centre of cool here, Brock. Even the few days suspension the guys already took could mean I'll be facing a first-class miserable time."

"I don't know, Sidney, but I don't think so. You didn't stick around to see how subdued the students were after the assembly. That's usually a sign that the message got through. I think you'll find more supporters in this school than you know."

"So is the suspension they served all the punishment they're getting?"

"Apart from the apologies? Pretty much. Since hearing the inconclusive results of the police investigation, VP Finning has fixed on the idea of this being a band stunt and she's said that she'll request the band be barred from performing at any school function in the city for so long as they're students in the system. If she goes ahead with it we won't know that decision for a month or so. It would be made at board level."

Sid gripped the desk and pushed so the chair swivelled. She stared out the window for a long time, her thoughts circling and circling.

Brock finally said, "I'm sorry you had to go through this, Sid. Do you want me to call your father in?"

"Not yet." Sid eyed a bee bouncing against the outside of the window screen – she'd been just like that, trying and trying to get into a place she wouldn't have liked in the end.

"Do you want to tell me how you're feeling? Saying it out loud can sometimes help your thoughts come together."

Sid considered that. "It's like I have three voices inside."

"What are they saying?"

"Well... One is quivering in the corner, wishing all this would just go away."

"That's pretty normal."

Sid turned the chair back to face Brock. "You like that word way too much." He smiled and shrugged. She gave him an exaggerated look of exasperation, then became serious. "One voice, the loudest, is saying I should let them all rot. Preferably in a cold dark cell full of rats. Not that that's a real option."

He nodded slowly and spoke the same way. "I'm not surprised, given how angry you've sounded this morning. So are you considering a civil suit?"

"Maybe. But..." She closed her eyes and tapped a swing rhythm on her shin.

"But what, Sid?"

"I have this friend, an old jazz musician from way back. He lived in New Orleans decades ago, and gradually migrated north, bit by bit, until he opened his club downtown. He's been trying to teach me to feel the beat. Last time I jammed with him I flipped it and to cover kicked into a drum solo. He doesn't think much of hard rock. Said I need to do more than just feel the beat. I need to 'control the flow so I don't start flailing like a chicken with its head chopped off'."

"A direct quote?"

Sid heard the amusement and nodded. "The thing is, this third voice is kind of quiet, but it feels like the beat. Like it's in my bones. I haven't heard it much these past few days because the loud voice has been wailing so loud. But the quiet voice is drumming along like a soft jazz riff."

"What does it say?"

Sid frowned. "What happens if I don't do the civil suit thing?"

Brock leaned forward. "There's still the board meeting. Those boys will be choked if their band is, ah, banned." He gave Sid an apologetic shrug for the bad pun.

"Clem was behind all this."

"Without proof..."

Sid sighed. "Right. And what about Wes? He was Clem's stooge. He was worse than me when it came to doing anything to get into the band."

"Normally I can't discuss other students with you. I think I can tell you that Wes discovered, the hard way, that his mother was a dedicated feminist lawyer before she cut back her number of clients to raise children. She deals mostly with businesses these days, but interestingly, they're mostly women-owned and operated."

Sid thought for a moment. "So he might be more than knee-deep in trouble at home?" No wonder he had looked so pathetic as he was leaving. Maybe she'd offer a truce so long as he treated her decently.

"Neck deep, at least. Believe me. I've already heard part of her, ah, re-education plan, which starts with not being allowed to join TFD."

It seemed only right to Sid that TFD came out of this without a drummer. She unfolded her legs off the chair and leaned forward. "That quiet voice, it kind of thinks life will run smoother if I just go with the flow."

"So you think it's fair that they get off free and clear? Rock basically assaulted you. Then what they did with that video..." Brock shook his head, as if to clear the images from his mind.

"Whose side are you on?"

"Yours."

Sid suppressed a smile. "Oh. Well, since you're so into honesty and that kind of crap, you should know I feel like I walked into that video mess when I knew better."

Brock raised his eyebrows and waited.

"I had a bad feeling about it as soon as I saw the guys were drinking – which was probably the quiet voice if I'd bothered to listen – but I still went up to Rock when he called me. I should've run right then. I didn't."

"That didn't give any of them the right to do what they did. Not the unwanted kiss and not that nasty innuendo at the end of the video." He lowered his voice. "Lack of evidence aside, sexual assault is very serious, Sid. You need to understand that that's what happened here."

"Yeah. I get it, Brock. I do. But they're being punished. Sort of. And I'm thinking that a civil suit would mean I'd have to testify in court and put Dad through even more days like this one. How's his ulcer supposed to get better if I keep this up? He won't go to a doctor no matter how much I nag. And I think the biggest thing to come from a law suit is that I'd become a target in school. Yeah, they were nasty, but I wasn't hurt, just humiliated. Believe me, it won't happen again."

Brock smiled. "You've got a smart quiet voice there, Sid. I hope you keep listening to it. What's it saying about not joining the band?"

"There are other bands. Maybe I'll even start my own. If I ask Sam at Downtown Music, I know she'd ask around for me, maybe help me find some interested musicians."

"That sounds like a good plan. But how's the loud voice feeling right now?"

"Madder than hell. Wants to go home and pound drums 'til they shatter."

"Will you?"

"No. I'm going to go home and practise a little jazz, and maybe 'Workin' Them Angels.' Something that makes me control the flow."

"So you're done with heavy metal?"

"No way." Sid grinned. "A girl's gotta let loose once in a while."

29 | crescendo

Sid and Brad stopped in the hallway outside the gymnasium. The decorations from the prom spilled out of the gym all the way to the main entrance, a jungle of huge potted plants interspersed with golden bouquets of helium-filled balloons nodding in time to the music. It almost didn't look like a school.

She reached up and adjusted Brad's new glasses. He'd surprised her with them tonight. They were rimless on the bottom and didn't hide his toe-curling blue eyes. She almost wished he'd kept the old glasses. Almost. "Tell me again how we ended up here."

He rolled those amazing blue eyes. "You just like hearing me admit what an idiot I was." She nodded and he laughed. "After you explained things and left, I couldn't stop thinking about you. I realized that the jerk who'd told me those lies about you and Taylor was the same jerk who'd hurt you other ways. I didn't want him to win so that's when I showed up on your doorstep grovelling like the undeserving peasant I am."

"Got to love a guy who knows his place."

"Yeah, well, you'll never know how much it costs a guy to face a dad who'd caught him in an awkward position with his daughter."

"Would a kiss make up for your humiliation?"

A throat cleared. They turned to face Mr. Brock. He was wearing a black tux and his glasses were nowhere to be seen. Sid whistled. "Brock! You look hot!"

"Yes, he does, doesn't he?" A woman snaked her arm through his and smiled at Sid, who felt heat stain her cheeks.

"Ah. Hi. You must be Mrs. Brock."

Still smiling, the woman nodded. Brock said, "I just wanted to tell you how nice *you* look, Sidney. And to shamelessly seek an introduction. Your date doesn't look familiar."

"Imported," Sid said. "Brad, this is Brock. I've told you about him. Though I don't think I've ever mentioned that he's the coolest teacher in school."

Brock raised his eyebrows. "Not a teacher, Sid."

Sid copied his expression. "That could explain the cool part, Brock."

He laughed, shook hands with Brad and led his wife into the darkened gym. Brad tugged on her arm and they followed. He whispered, "I'm glad you wore the blue dress again, Sid. You really do look great in it."

"Thanks, but I'm done following Heather's fashion advice."

"You're going back to baggy?"

"No, but from now on I'm going to listen to the quiet

voice, even when it comes to fashion."

He didn't ask for an explanation, just took her hand and led her onto the dance floor where they spent the next hour. A slow dance started. Brad gathered her into his arms and said, "About time."

A moment later another couple interrupted. Narain and – Sid blinked – Joanne. Narain asked if they could switch partners. Brad sighed but relented. Before they could react, Narain grabbed Brad and twirled him away. Joanne stepped close and assumed lead in a traditional waltz position.

Slightly stunned by the speed of it all, Sid let herself be swept away. After a moment she said, "This feels...really awkward."

"It does," Joanne replied. "But it seemed like the only way I could get your attention to ask you something."

"Okay..." Sid trailed off, bemused. Joanne was a decent dancer but she could feel eyes following their progress and it was hard not to bolt.

Joanne said, "Is the boyfriend for real?"

Sid hesitated. They weren't officially a couple, but she knew Brad liked her as much as she liked him. "Yeah. He's real."

"Good." Joanne seemed to be guiding them toward the edge of the dance floor. "I want you to know that I'm really sorry about what happened at that party. Wes's girlfriend, ex-girlfriend, told me you were interested. I thought she was a friend. I'd never have..."

"It's okay, Joanne. Everybody made their share of bad

choices in that mess. Even me." Sid caught a glimpse of Brad, standing beside Narain and scowling as he watched her. "But the boyfriend wasn't one of them. Could we...?"

Joanne released her. "The offer I made in the library to be friends? It still stands."

"I think I'd like that." Sid tilted her head. "You don't play an instrument, do you?"

Joanne heaved a long-suffering sigh. "My mom made me take piano lessons."

"What level?"

"I have my Grade Eight."

"That's decent. Ever considered joining a band?"

"You're in a band that needs a keyboard player?"

"I'm starting a band. All-girl, I hope. Show those guys how rock is meant to be played."

Joanne smiled. "Sounds like it could be fun. I'll let you know." She walked away.

Sid headed toward Narain. She gave him a soft punch in the stomach and he exaggerated doubling over. Then he straightened and said, "Are you coming with me when I visit Taylor tomorrow?"

"You know I am, jerk." She gave him a smile and turned to Brad. "Could we get some fresh air?"

He nodded and took her hand. "Should I say you made a nice couple?"

"No."

They slipped out a side door, past Mr. Franklin who was bobbing out of time to the music. He nodded and waved them through.

They walked far enough to get away from the light spilling out of the doorway.

"So what did she want?" Brad asked, his voice a little tight.

"To be my friend. And to know if you were real."

"Huh?"

"You know, a real boyfriend."

A smile entered his voice. "Am I?"

"I don't know. Kiss me and help me make up my mind."

Long moments later, they came up for air. Sid laughed. "I think my knees are wobbly."

"Let's sit."

They ended up lying down, ear to ear, heads snugged against shoulders, staring up at the stars. "Wow," Sid said, "They're just as bright as the night of the wedding."

"Make a wish."

"That only counts with the first star. This sky has more stars than my dress has polka dots."

"Make a wish anyway."

Sid's hand reached up to find Brad's waiting for her. She interwove her fingers with his, enjoying the warmth. She could almost hear a heartbeat. And she was sure she could feel the rhythm of the earth rising in a soft insistent pulse that thrummed in her bones. "I wish, hope, that you'll be better at remembering my birthday than my dad is."

"When is it?"

"Ten days."

"Crap. You need to give a guy more warning."

She squeezed his hand. "What are you going to get me?"

"Oh sure, put me on the spot."

Sid watched the stars and let the rhythm flow through her. She didn't really expect Brad to answer. She was just enjoying the moment.

After a long pause he said, "I'm going to use my little sister's tye-dying kit and make you a tye-dyed T-shirt. And then I'll use her fabric markers to plaster it with words."

Sid shifted and raised up on her elbow so she was looking down into Brad's face. "Words? What kind of words?"

"Ones that tell what's special about you. A big one over your heart will read *Drummer Girl.* Smaller ones will say things like *Sister, Daughter, Friend, Carpenter,* maybe *Jazz Lover, Metalhead, Rocker Chick.* And in legal-sized print, on the bottom at the back, it will read..." He cleared his throat and licked his lips. *"Math Geek's Girlfriend?"*

Sid's heart picked up the tempo, just a little. "Sounds cool. There's only one problem."

"What's that."

"That last one? Way too small. It needs to be in larger print and right in the middle of a blue splotch that matches the geek's eyes."

"That can be arranged."

"Good. Do it."

He did.

acknowledgements

I can pick out a tune on a piano with one finger but don't actually play any musical instruments, except, once upon a time, the recorder. So many thanks to Kaleb Penner for answering all sorts of odd questions about being a drummer. Thanks, also, to Dymphny Dronyk for being my first reader, and for allowing me to glimpse the world of high school bands through her musical sons (though my band in no way resembles them)

This book is as you see it because of the dedication and hard work of all the wonderful people at Coteau Books – thank you to Nik, Susan, Amber, and everyone else who helped along the way. A special thank you to my editor, Laura Peetoom, for her keen insight and for throwing me a metaphoric lifeline when I needed it.

Finally, thanks to my husband, Michael, who encourages my daydreams and urges me to contine working at turning them into reality.